Mama Mia It's Murder

Excerpt:

The sea breeze ruffled Carmella Moretti's long, wavy hair as she stepped out of her car. The salty air mingled with a hint of pine from the surrounding woods, a sharp contrast to the exhaust fumes of New York City she was accustomed to. Her eyes darted across Wavecrest Cove's main street, lined with pastel-colored shop fronts and hanging flower baskets swaying gently. Excitement fluttered in her chest, a butterfly trapped but ready to soar.

She locked the car with a beep, her petite frame poised at the edge of change. A seagull's cry punctuated the moment, and she turned her gaze towards "Nonna's Slice of Heaven" down the cobblestone path. Its red-and-white striped awning beckoned, a beacon of nostalgia wrapped in promise.

Carmella's stylish sneakers clicked rhythmically against the stone, her pace quickening with each step. Her expressive eyes, once scanning apprehensively, now narrowed with resolve. She reached for the brass door handle, its coolness grounding her swirling thoughts. This was it—the threshold of legacy and future. A surge of excitement pulsed through her veins; she was ready to make it a success.

The bell above the door chimed as Carmella stepped into the dimly lit pizzeria. Warmth enveloped her, a stark contrast to the brisk coastal air outside. The rich, yeasty scent of dough baking in the stone oven flooded her senses. Her heart skipped; memories of kneading dough at her grandfather's side.

"Grandpa," she muttered, her voice laced with nostalgia.

"Ah, you must be Carmella! Welcome to Wavecrest Cove, dear!"

The voice boomed from the entrance, slicing through the veil of reminiscence. Carmella turned toward the figure framed by the doorway. Sunlight haloed Mayor Edna Perkins, her silver bob a shining cap against the bright sky. Her glasses caught the light, obscuring her eyes for a moment before she stepped inside, casting colorful shadows on the checkered floor.

"Mayor Edna!" Carmella exclaimed, recognizing the town's emblematic figure from the newsletters her grandfather used to pin to the fridge.

Edna's laughter filled the space, a melody that seemed to resonate with the building's very walls. She closed the distance between them in a few enthusiastic strides, her chunky jewelry clinking with each step.

A smile spread across Carmella's face, mirroring the boundless joy that seemed to radiate from Mayor Edna. The warmth in the room was no longer just from the oven. "Thank you, Mayor Edna. It's an honor to be here," she said, her voice steady with a gratitude that reached beyond mere politeness.

"Come, come!" Edna beckoned, her voice as vibrant as the scarf draped around her neck. She clasped Carmella's hand, the grip firm and reassuring. Together, they wove through the maze of tables, laughter and conversations ebbing and flowing around them like waves against the cove's shore.

The corner booth awaited, its cushions well-worn from years of patrons forging memories over slices of pizza. They settled in, the leather giving a soft sigh under their weight. Edna's eyes were bright, her magnified gaze locked onto Carmella with an intensity that brimmed with expectation and excitement.

The door creaked open, a cool breeze flirting with the scent of tomato and basil. Greta Olsen, bearing her trademark smile, sauntered in. Her eyes locked on Carmella.

"Well, well, if it isn't our newest pizza queen," Greta's voice danced through the air, playful, light. "Heard you're here to shake things up, huh?"

Carmella's lips curved into a chuckle, her heart buoyed by the warmth in Greta's tease. "That's the plan, Greta. I want to honor my family's legacy and bring Nonna's Slice of Heaven back to its former glory."

Greta nodded, her blonde hair catching the dim light. She leaned closer, conspiratorial, her glasses slipping just so. The clink of her bracelets punctuated the moment, a silent cheer for Carmella's resolve.

Mayor Edna's eyes sparkled as she leaned forward, her voice a whisper of shared secrets and high hopes. "Wavecrest Cove has missed the magic of your grandfather's pizza, Carmella. We're counting on you to bring it back!"

Carmella inhaled, the scent of oregano and melted cheese wrapping around her like a comforting embrace. She looked around the pizzeria, at the faded checkered tablecloths, the walls adorned with old family photos, and the wood-fired oven's steady glow. In that moment, the place hummed with silent promises, each empty seat an echo of laughter and camaraderie yet to come.

Her heart thrummed a steady beat, a metronome to her newfound resolve. She could see it — the future painted in vibrant strokes of life and community, where every night the pizzeria buzzed with the energy of hungry patrons and the air swirled with the aroma of freshly baked pies.

"Envisioning the rush already?" Mayor Edna asked, her tone light, knowing.

Carmella nodded, a smile breaking across her face. "Exactly that, Mayor. It's going to be wonderful." Her voice carried the weight of her determination, the sound of it mingling seamlessly with the muted clatter of dishes from the kitchen, a symphony of beginnings.

Mayor Edna's scarf fluttered as she gestured animatedly, her voice a melody of nostalgia and pride. "Every summer, the air fills with the scent of competition. It's not just about the pizza; it's tradition, camaraderie."

"Indeed," Greta chimed in, her glasses catching the light as she leaned closer. "The Bake-off Festival. Families gather, recipes secret as buried treasure. Ovens ablaze from dawn till dusk."

Carmella's fingers tapped the tabletop, her mind alight with visions of dough spinning under her hands, sauce simmering with spices. She pictured the pizzeria's walls echoing with the buzz of excited voices, judges sampling slices with discerning eyes.

"Flames leap, crusts golden," Mayor Edna continued, her hands mimicking the dance of fire. "The winner's pie becomes legend for a year."

"Nonna's Slice could reign once more." Greta's wink was conspiratorial, an unspoken challenge hanging between them.

"Imagine that," Carmella said, her pulse quickening at the thought. The legacy of her grandfather mingling with her own dreams, a future intertwined with Wavecrest Cove's beating heart.

"Your touch could tip the scales," Mayor Edna mused, her gaze fixed on Carmella with an unwavering belief.

"Could tip them indeed," Carmella replied, her resolve crystallizing into action. She saw it now—a path woven through trial and taste, a quest to stir the soul of the town with a blend of old and new.

"Bring your spirit, Carmella," Greta said, nodding sagely. "Let Wavecrest Cove taste your passion."

"Let them taste it," Carmella echoed. Her grandfather's legacy would live on, not just in memory, but in every bite savored under the roof of Nonna's Slice of Heaven.

Carmella leaned in, her gaze sweeping across the familiar checkered tablecloths and the glossy varnish of the pizzeria's wooden booths. Mayor Edna's stories wove a tapestry of community spirit, each thread pulling at Carmella's heart.

"Last year's Bake-off," the mayor said, voice low with reverence, "brought out every secret recipe in town."

"Secrets are the lifeblood here," Greta chimed in, tapping a finger against her temple. Her eyes twinkled with the same mischief that laced her words.

The clink of glasses and the murmur of conversation from other tables filled the space between stories. Carmella felt the room's energy seeping into her bones, warm and invigorating. The scent of oregano hung in the air, a fragrant reminder of her new reality.

"Seems I've got my work cut out for me," Carmella mused aloud. Her hands folded over one another, steady and sure.

"Cut out, indeed," Mayor Edna replied with a nod. "But you've got the town behind you."

Carmella's shoulders relaxed. A smile tugged at the corners of her mouth as she absorbed the friendships, family and coziness, the collective breath of Wavecrest Cove she always remembered.

"Nonna's Slice has always been more than just pizza," Greta said, leaning back in her seat. "It's a landmark, a memory maker."

"Memory maker huh?" Carmella repeated softly. The words settled around her like a promise, a mantle she was ready to wear.

"Exactly," Mayor Edna affirmed. "You're not just filling bellies. You're stitching together the fabric of our little society."

Book List

Accidental Vows
Spectres and Souffles
Hex and the City
Pies and Perps
Cabinet of Curiosities
Love in Stitches
Sin Takes a Holiday
Better off Dead
The Gingerdead Men
Welcome to Scarecrow Hollow
The Boogeyman
The Pendleton Witches

Patti Petrone Miller

Mamma Mia It's Murder

Garlic Bread Recipe

Ingredients:

- 1 baguette or Italian bread loaf
- 1/2 cup (113g) unsalted butter, softened
- 4 cloves garlic, minced
- 2 tablespoons fresh parsley, finely chopped
- 1/4 cup (25g) grated Parmesan cheese
- Salt to taste

Instructions:

1. Preheat your oven to 350°F (175°C).
2. Cut the bread into slices, about 1 inch thick, without cutting all the way through the bottom crust.
3. In a bowl, mix the softened butter, minced garlic, chopped parsley, Parmesan cheese, and a pinch of salt.
4. Spread the butter mixture between each slice of bread.
5. Wrap the entire loaf in aluminum foil.
6. Bake for 15-20 minutes until the butter is melted and the bread is warm.
7. Unwrap and bake for an additional 5 minutes to crisp up the crust.

Pizza Recipes

1. Classic Margherita Pizza

Ingredients:

- 1 pizza dough (homemade or store-bought)
- 1/2 cup (120ml) tomato sauce
- 8 oz (225g) fresh mozzarella, sliced
- Fresh basil leaves
- 2 tablespoons extra virgin olive oil

- Salt to taste

Instructions:
1. Preheat your oven to 450°F (230°C) with a pizza stone if you have one.
2. Roll out the pizza dough on a floured surface.
3. Spread the tomato sauce evenly over the dough.
4. Add sliced mozzarella.
5. Bake for 12-15 minutes until the crust is golden and the cheese is bubbly.
6. Remove from the oven and top with fresh basil leaves, a drizzle of olive oil, and a pinch of salt.

2. BBQ Chicken Pizza

Ingredients:
- 1 pizza dough
- 1/2 cup (120ml) BBQ sauce
- 1 1/2 cups (170g) cooked chicken, shredded
- 1 cup (100g) shredded mozzarella cheese
- 1/4 red onion, thinly sliced
- 1/4 cup (25g) chopped fresh cilantro

Instructions:
1. Preheat your oven to 450°F (230°C).
2. Roll out the pizza dough.
3. Spread BBQ sauce over the dough.
4. Top with shredded chicken, mozzarella cheese, and red onion slices.
5. Bake for 12-15 minutes until the crust is golden and the cheese is melted.
6. Sprinkle with fresh cilantro before serving.

3. Vegetarian Supreme Pizza

Ingredients:

- 1 pizza dough
- 1/2 cup (120ml) tomato sauce
- 1 1/2 cups (150g) shredded mozzarella cheese
- 1/2 cup (50g) sliced bell peppers
- 1/2 cup (50g) sliced red onions
- 1/2 cup (50g) sliced mushrooms
- 1/4 cup (25g) sliced black olives
- 1 tablespoon dried oregano

Instructions:

1. Preheat your oven to 450°F (230°C).
2. Roll out the pizza dough.
3. Spread tomato sauce over the dough.
4. Sprinkle half of the mozzarella cheese.
5. Add bell peppers, red onions, mushrooms, and black olives.
6. Top with remaining cheese and sprinkle with dried oregano.
7. Bake for 12-15 minutes until the crust is golden and the cheese is bubbly.

Patti Petrone Miller

Copyright © 2024 Patti Petrone Miller All rights reserved

The characters and events portrayed in this book are fictitious. Any similarity to real persons, living or dead, is coincidental and not intended by the author.

No part of this book may be reproduced, or stored in a retrieval system, or transmitted in any form or by any means, electronic, mechanical, photocopying, recording, or otherwise, without express written permission of the publisher.

Cover design by: TMT Book Cover Desgins
Printed in Las Vegas Nevada
isbn: **9798343248241**

For my Beloved Tessa

Meet the Characters:

- **Carmella Moretti** Age: 32 Occupation: Former New York advertising executive, now owner of Nonna's Slice of Heaven pizzeria Appearance: Petite with wavy brown hair and expressive dark eyes Personality: Determined, quick-witted, optimistic Background: Born and raised in New York City, granddaughter of Italian immigrants Key traits: Creative problem-solver, loyal to family legacy, adapting to small-town life Character arc: From big-city skeptic to small-town defender and amateur sleuth
- **Detective Maddox Jones** Age: 38 Occupation: Wavecrest Cove Police Detective Appearance: Tall, athletic build, short dark hair, piercing blue eyes Personality: Skeptical, methodical, initially reserved but warms up to Carmella Background: Moved to Wavecrest Cove from a larger city police force Key traits: Sharp observational skills, dry sense of humor, commitment to justice Character arc: From lone wolf investigator to community protector and romantic partner
- **Kathleen Murray** Age: 34 Occupation: Librarian at Wavecrest Cove Public Library Appearance: Tall, slender, with fiery red hair and green eyes Personality: Intelligent, witty, supportive friend Background: Lifelong Wavecrest Cove resident, history buff Key traits: Excellent researcher, loyal friend, voice of reason Role: Carmella's best friend and amateur investigation partner
- **Otto Marks** Age: 55 Occupation: Owner of rival pizzeria, Marks of Excellence Appearance: Lean, balding with thin-rimmed glasses Personality: Ambitious, cunning, outwardly charming Background: Second-generation pizzeria owner in Wavecrest Cove Key traits: Competitive, secretive, manipulative Role: Primary antagonist and murder suspect

- **Mayor Edna Perkins** Age: 68 Occupation: Mayor of Wavecrest Cove Appearance: Short silver bob, colorful scarves, glasses Personality: Energetic, gossipy, well-meaning Background: Born and raised in Wavecrest Cove, longtime public servant Key traits: Knows everyone's business, community cheerleader, occasionally meddlesome Role: Local color and occasional source of information
- **Frankie "The Dough" Marino** Age: 60 Occupation: Retired pizzaiolo, local pizza legend Appearance: Robust build, salt-and-pepper curls, always wearing an apron Personality: Boisterous, generous, passionate about pizza Background: Third-generation Italian-American, mentored by Carmella's grandfather Key traits: Master of pizza dough, storyteller, protective of Carmella Role: Mentor figure and link to Carmella's family history

Patti Petrone Miller

Chapter 1

The sea breeze ruffled Carmella Moretti's long, wavy hair as she stepped out of her car. The salty air mingled with a hint of pine from the surrounding woods, a sharp contrast to the exhaust fumes of New York City she was accustomed to. Her eyes darted across Wavecrest Cove's main street, lined with pastel-colored shop fronts and hanging flower baskets swaying gently. Excitement fluttered in her chest, a butterfly trapped but ready to soar.

She locked the car with a beep, her petite frame poised at the edge of change. A seagull's cry punctuated the moment, and she turned her gaze towards "Nonna's Slice of Heaven" down the cobblestone path. Its red-and-white striped awning beckoned, a beacon of nostalgia wrapped in promise.

Carmella's stylish sneakers clicked rhythmically against the stone, her pace quickening with each step. Her expressive eyes, once scanning apprehensively, now narrowed with resolve. She reached for the brass door handle, its coolness grounding her swirling thoughts. This was it— the threshold of legacy and future. A surge of excitement pulsed through her veins; she was ready to make it a success.

The bell above the door chimed as Carmella stepped into the dimly lit pizzeria. Warmth enveloped her, a stark contrast to the brisk coastal air outside. The rich, yeasty scent of dough baking in the stone oven flooded her senses. Her heart skipped; memories of kneading dough at her grandfather's side.

"Grandpa," she muttered, her voice laced with nostalgia.

"Ah, you must be Carmella! Welcome to Wavecrest Cove, dear!"

The voice boomed from the entrance, slicing through the veil of reminiscence. Carmella turned toward the figure framed by the doorway. Sunlight haloed Mayor Edna Perkins, her silver bob a shining cap against the bright sky. Her glasses caught the light, obscuring her eyes for a moment before she stepped inside, casting colorful shadows on the checkered floor.

"Mayor Edna!" Carmella exclaimed, recognizing the town's emblematic figure from the newsletters her grandfather used to pin to the fridge.

Edna's laughter filled the space, a melody that seemed to resonate with the building's very walls. She closed the distance between them in a few enthusiastic strides, her chunky jewelry clinking with each step.

A smile spread across Carmella's face, mirroring the boundless joy that seemed to radiate from Mayor Edna. The warmth in the room was no longer just from the oven. "Thank you, Mayor Edna. It's an honor to be here," she said, her voice steady with a gratitude that reached beyond mere politeness.

"Come, come!" Edna beckoned, her voice as vibrant as the scarf draped around her neck. She clasped Carmella's hand, the grip firm and reassuring. Together, they wove through the maze of tables, laughter and conversations ebbing and flowing around them like waves against the cove's shore.

The corner booth awaited, its cushions well-worn from years of patrons forging memories over slices of pizza. They settled in, the leather giving a soft sigh under their weight. Edna's eyes were bright, her magnified gaze locked onto Carmella with an intensity that brimmed with expectation and excitement.

The door creaked open, a cool breeze flirting with the scent of tomato and basil. Greta Olsen, bearing her trademark smile, sauntered in. Her eyes locked on Carmella.

"Well, well, if it isn't our newest pizza queen," Greta's voice danced through the air, playful, light. "Heard you're here to shake things up, huh?"

Carmella's lips curved into a chuckle, her heart buoyed by the warmth in Greta's tease. "That's the plan, Greta. I want to honor my family's legacy and bring Nonna's Slice of Heaven back to its former glory."

Greta nodded, her blonde hair catching the dim light. She leaned closer, conspiratorial, her glasses slipping just so. The clink of her bracelets punctuated the moment, a silent cheer for Carmella's resolve.

Mayor Edna's eyes sparkled as she leaned forward, her voice a whisper of shared secrets and high hopes. "Wavecrest Cove has missed the magic of your grandfather's pizza, Carmella. We're counting on you to bring it back!"

Carmella inhaled, the scent of oregano and melted cheese wrapping around her like a comforting embrace. She looked around the pizzeria, at the faded checkered tablecloths, the walls adorned with old family photos, and the wood-fired oven's steady glow. In that moment, the place hummed with silent promises, each empty seat an echo of laughter and camaraderie yet to come.

Her heart thrummed a steady beat, a metronome to her newfound resolve. She could see it — the future painted in vibrant strokes of life and community, where every night the pizzeria buzzed with the energy of hungry patrons and the air swirled with the aroma of freshly baked pies.

"Envisioning the rush already?" Mayor Edna asked, her tone light, knowing.

Carmella nodded, a smile breaking across her face. "Exactly that, Mayor. It's going to be wonderful." Her voice carried the weight of her determination, the sound of it mingling seamlessly with the muted clatter of dishes from the kitchen, a symphony of beginnings.

Mayor Edna's scarf fluttered as she gestured animatedly, her voice a melody of nostalgia and pride. "Every summer, the air fills with the scent of competition. It's not just about the pizza; it's tradition, camaraderie."

"Indeed," Greta chimed in, her glasses catching the light as she leaned closer. "The Bake-off Festival. Families gather, recipes secret as buried treasure. Ovens ablaze from dawn till dusk."

Carmella's fingers tapped the tabletop, her mind alight with visions of dough spinning under her hands, sauce simmering with spices. She pictured the pizzeria's walls echoing with the buzz of excited voices, judges sampling slices with discerning eyes.

"Flames leap, crusts golden," Mayor Edna continued, her hands mimicking the dance of fire. "The winner's pie becomes legend for a year."

"Nonna's Slice could reign once more." Greta's wink was conspiratorial, an unspoken challenge hanging between them.

"Imagine that," Carmella said, her pulse quickening at the thought. The legacy of her grandfather mingling with her own dreams, a future intertwined with Wavecrest Cove's beating heart.

"Your touch could tip the scales," Mayor Edna mused, her gaze fixed on Carmella with an unwavering belief.

"Could tip them indeed," Carmella replied, her resolve crystallizing into action. She saw it now—a path woven through trial and taste, a quest to stir the soul of the town with a blend of old and new.

"Bring your spirit, Carmella," Greta said, nodding sagely. "Let Wavecrest Cove taste your passion."

"Let them taste it," Carmella echoed. Her grandfather's legacy would live on, not just in memory, but in every bite savored under the roof of Nonna's Slice of Heaven.

Carmella leaned in, her gaze sweeping across the familiar checkered tablecloths and the glossy varnish of the pizzeria's wooden booths. Mayor Edna's stories wove a tapestry of community spirit, each thread pulling at Carmella's heart.

"Last year's Bake-off," the mayor said, voice low with reverence, "brought out every secret recipe in town."

"Secrets are the lifeblood here," Greta chimed in, tapping a finger against her temple. Her eyes twinkled with the same mischief that laced her words.

The clink of glasses and the murmur of conversation from other tables filled the space between stories. Carmella felt the room's energy seeping into her bones, warm and invigorating. The scent of oregano hung in the air, a fragrant reminder of her new reality.

"Seems I've got my work cut out for me," Carmella mused aloud. Her hands folded over one another, steady and sure.

"Cut out, indeed," Mayor Edna replied with a nod. "But you've got the town behind you."

Carmella's shoulders relaxed. A smile tugged at the corners of her mouth as she absorbed the friendships, family and coziness, the collective breath of Wavecrest Cove she always remembered.

"Nonna's Slice has always been more than just pizza," Greta said, leaning back in her seat. "It's a landmark, a memory maker."

"Memory maker huh?" Carmella repeated softly. The words settled around her like a promise, a mantle she was ready to wear.

"Exactly," Mayor Edna affirmed. "You're not just filling bellies. You're stitching together the fabric of our little society."

"Stitch by stitch," Carmella said, her commitment threading through her voice. Her initial trepidation had dissolved, leaving a clear-eyed vision of her path forward.

"Stitch by stitch," the mayor echoed, raising her glass in a silent toast to the future.

Carmella mirrored the gesture, her glass catching the fading sunlight that streamed through the window. She belonged here, amongst these people, their lives interlaced with her own.

"Wavecrest Cove won't know what hit it," Greta declared, a grin spreading across her face.

"Let's hope they're ready," Carmella said, her laughter mingling with the hum of the pizzeria. Her heart swelled, full of the stories yet to be written on this coastal canvas.

Chapter 2

Carmella's breath caught as the chill of the walk-in freezer nipped at her skin, a stark contrast to the warmth of the pizzeria kitchen she'd just left. She reached for a sack of flour, her movements habitual and assured until her eyes landed on an unnerving sight. There, beneath the hanging sides of cured meats and shelves laden with fresh vegetables, lay Tony Bianco—immobile on the cold floor, his face pale against the frost. A gasp tore from Carmella's lips, a sound swallowed by the hum of the freezer. Her hand flew to her mouth, fingertips pressing against her lips to stifle a scream that threatened to erupt. The jovial Tony she knew, with his boisterous laugh and flamboyant gestures, was reduced to silence, his larger-than-life personality extinguished.

"Tony?" Her voice emerged as a hoarse whisper, disbelief lacing each syllable. No response came from the still figure on the ground. Carmella's heart hammered in her chest, a rhythm that quickened with the realization of the grim tableau before her. This man, who had been both adversary and part of Wavecrest Cove's culinary fabric, now lay as lifeless as the slabs of meat surrounding him.

She took a step back, her foot nudging a bag of onions that rolled away with a soft thud. The need to flee wrestled with her resolve, but it was her dedication to Nonna's Slice of Heaven and the town itself that anchored her to the spot. She could not turn away; this was more than a chilling discovery—it was a call to defend her family's honor and seek the truth for poor Tony.

"Okay, Carmella," she muttered to herself, her voice barely audible above the freezer's relentless drone. "Think, you're going to be the prime suspect." Her mind raced, piecing together the last time she saw Tony, alive and vibrant, tossing dough in his own establishment, a temple to his own legacy. Now he was here, in her domain, silenced forever. Who would do this?

Terrified and shaken she managed to yell help, knowing she needed to act swiftly. Time was of the essence, and every second lost could mean the difference between justice for Tony and a stain on her grandfather's cherished pizzeria and her own name.

Carmella's pulse pounded in her ears, a deafening reminder of the horror just inches away. She stumbled backward, her movements jagged with panic. Her shoulder collided with a towering stack of pizza boxes that teetered for a moment before cascading to the ground in a chaotic symphony of cardboard and white paper.

"Someone—anyone!" The cry tore from her throat as she lurched towards the freezer door, her hands trembling so violently it took her three attempts to heave it open. Cold air rushed past her, dissipating into the warmth of the kitchen as she emerged, breathless and wild-eyed.

Moments later, the bell above Nonna's entrance tinkled its usual cheerful greeting, an absurd contrast to the scene unfolding within. Detective Maddox Jones stepped over the threshold, his blue eyes scanning the pizzeria with practiced precision. He moved with deliberate steps, the very image of cool composure amidst the chaos. "I heard someone calling for help all the way outside. Was it you?"

"Detective Jones," Carmella managed to say, her voice a thin thread of sound.

"Ms. Moretti." His acknowledgment was curt but concerned, his gaze taking in her disheveled appearance—the flour on her apron, her hair escaping its tie in frantic wisps.

"Freezer," she gasped out, pointing shakily towards the stainless steel door now hanging ajar.

Maddox's brow furrowed as he moved past her, pausing only to glance at the toppled boxes. Every step was methodical, his presence a steadying force within the turmoil. As he disappeared into the cold chamber, Carmella wrapped her arms around herself, fighting off a shiver that had nothing to do with the temperature.

Maddox emerged from the freezer, his expression unreadable. Ice crystals clung to the edges of his coat. He approached Carmella, eyes sharp and probing.

"Ms. Moretti," he started, his voice even, "when did you find Mr. Bianco?"

Carmella's heart thundered against her ribs. She straightened up, tightening the grip on her own arms. "Just now!" she said, meeting his gaze. "I—I just wanted to prep for the day."

"Alone?" Maddox asked, one eyebrow arching ever so slightly.

"Always am." Her words were quick, defensive. "The crew doesn't come in until later." She searched his face for a sign, any sign, that he believed her.

"Anyone else know you're here at this time?" The detective's tone remained steady, his eyes flicking briefly to the doorway as if imagining the scene playing out.

"Only my staff," she replied. "And now Tony..." Her voice broke on the last word, but she caught herself, a fresh wave of emotions washing over her features. "But I didn't do this, Detective. I loved this place. My grandfather's legacy means everything to me."

Maddox nodded slowly, jotting something down in his notepad. "Understandable," he murmured, though the skepticism lingered in the set of his jaw.

"Please, you have to believe me," Carmella implored, desperation threading through her plea. "Tony and I—we were rivals, yes, but never... This is insane. I just found him like that! You think I did this?"

"Rivalries can turn bitter." His words were noncommittal, but they hung between them, heavy with implication.

"Not this bitter." Carmella's fists clenched at her sides. "I would never harm anyone."

"Of course," Maddox said, closing his notepad with a soft snap. His scrutiny didn't waver, though it seemed to soften around the edges. "We'll need to ask more questions, Ms. Moretti. It's procedure."

"Ask away." Her chin lifted, a gesture of both challenge and courage. "I want to help. I need to clear my name."

"Good," Maddox responded, a hint of approval in his tone. He glanced back once more at the freezer door, still slightly ajar. "That's exactly what we'll do."

Maddox Jones pushed open the freezer door, a blast of cold air greeting him as he stepped back inside with other officers following behind.. The sharp scent of basil and tomatoes was undercut by something metallic, something that didn't belong in this icy tomb. He crouched beside Tony Bianco's lifeless body, his eyes scanning for any out-of-place detail—a misplaced tool, a scuff on the floor, anything.

"Touch nothing," he said, his voice echoing slightly off the walls lined with shelves of cheese and pepperoni. He pulled out his camera, snapping photos from every angle, documenting the scene before the coroner would whisk Tony away.

Carmella stood just outside, her arms wrapped tightly around herself as if to ward off a chill that had settled deep in her bones. Her gaze followed Maddox's every move, while her mind spun wildly with thoughts of what Tony's death could mean for Nonna's Slice of Heaven. A rivalry turned murder would be town gossip for months, casting shadows where there had once been the warm glow of oven lights.

The detective straightened up, pulling a small flashlight from his pocket. He flicked it on, the beam cutting through the freezer's artificial twilight. It danced over racks of dough, tubs of sauce, finally pausing on a cluster of frozen herbs that had spilled to the floor.

"Accident or intention?" he muttered to himself, stooping to inspect the green flecks now crystallized in ice. His fingers brushed over a nearby shelf, coming away with a fine dusting of flour.

"Detective?" Carmella's voice broke through his concentration. "If you think I had anything to do with this..."

"Every possibility is on the table, Ms. Moretti," he replied without looking up, his tone firm but not unkind. "It's my job to sift through them."

Carmella nodded, biting down on her lower lip. She watched him work, her heart pounding a relentless rhythm. This place was more than a pizzeria; it was her sanctuary, her connection to a family she longed to honor. The thought of losing it, or worse, being blamed for such a horror, tightened a vice around her chest.

"Find who did this," she whispered, almost to herself. "For Tony. For Nonna's."

Maddox stood, giving the room one last sweeping glance before stepping out of the freezer. He met Carmella's eyes, finding a flicker of something he recognized—fear..

"Trust the process, Ms. Moretti," he said. "We'll get to the bottom of this." He then moved past her, his footsteps steady and sure as he made his way to question the staff, leaving Carmella with her thoughts and the growing weight of uncertainty.

Carmella's hands trembled. The shock had worn off. She couldn't stand idle, not with her life's work at stake. Tony's death—a brutal mystery in the heart of her world—demanded action. Her grandfather's legacy deserved that much.

Detective Jones was deep in conversation with one of her waitstaff when Carmella approached. She squared her shoulders, drawing from a well of courage she hadn't known existed. "Detective," she said, her voice clear and steady despite the chaos swirling within.

He turned, his eyes locking onto hers. A silent question hovered between them.

"I know this place. I know the people," she continued, her gaze unwavering. "I want to help. I need to help."

A pause. He studied her, considering the offer. His nod was slight, almost imperceptible.

"Let's hear what you've got," he said, folding his arms across his chest. It wasn't an embrace of partnership, but it wasn't a dismissal either.

Carmella exhaled, the breath she didn't realize she'd been holding. She launched into details, recounting interactions, highlighting quirks of regulars, sketching the web of relationships that made up Wavecrest Cove's culinary scene. Every word painted her as an insider, invaluable to threading through the tangled motives that could lurk behind Tony's death.

"Alright, Ms. Moretti," Detective Jones finally said, jotting notes in his pad. "Let's see where this goes."

Detective Jones' eyes narrowed as he regarded Carmella, weighing her offer against an ingrained caution. She stood firm, the set of her jaw and the earnest plea in her eyes spoke volumes. The detective's mind turned over the possibilities; her intimate knowledge of the community could be an asset.

"Fine," he conceded, a grudging respect taking root. "But you follow my lead."

Carmella nodded, relief washing over her. They moved through Nonna's Slice of Heaven, the din of conversation and clinking silverware filling the space.

"Start with Rosa," Carmella pointed to a waitress balancing plates of steaming pizza. Detective Jones stepped forward, his presence commanding immediate attention.

"Ms. Rosa, when did you last see Tony Bianco?" His voice cut through the bustle.

"Two days ago," Rosa replied, wiping her hands on her apron. Her eyes darted to Carmella, then back to the detective.

"Anyone unusual around? Any arguments?"

Rosa shook her head. "Just the usual crowd."

They pressed on, questioning patrons nestled in red vinyl booths, their faces a mix of curiosity and concern. Each answer seemed to lead nowhere, adding to the ambiguity of the situation. Carmella's persistence never wavered, her questions pointed, revealing an intricate map of personal ties.

"Could anyone here benefit from Tony's... absence?" Carmella asked a regular, Mr. Sullivan, who nursed his third espresso.

"Benefit?" He stroked his chin thoughtfully. "Well, there's talk of the food festival. Big opportunity for exposure."

Detective Jones scribbled in his notebook, his gaze sharp. "Talk?"

"Tony was boastful. Said this year, he'd outshine everyone," Mr. Sullivan continued, a furrow forming on his brow.

"Boastful enough to make enemies?" Detective Jones pressed.

"Maybe," admitted Mr. Sullivan, sipping his drink.

The afternoon waned, shadows stretching across the floor. Each inquiry peeled back layers, exposing threads of rivalry, ambition, jealousy. Carmella's insights guided them, her familiarity with the townsfolk proving invaluable. The detective's initial reluctance had evolved into a silent acknowledgment of her contributions.

"Seems we have more digging to do," he muttered, closing his notebook.

Carmella met his gaze. "I'm ready."

Carmella sifted through stacks of delivery invoices, her fingers stained with ink and dust. Detective Jones watched from a distance, his arms crossed as he leaned against the stainless steel prep table. His eyes followed Carmella's every move, analyzing, considering.

"Look at this," Carmella said, holding up a crinkled paper. "Tony ordered an unusual amount of exotic ingredients last week."

"Exotic?" Jones echoed, approaching to take the invoice.

"Truffles, saffron, caviar," Carmella listed off, tapping the paper. "Not his usual fare for a simple slice shop."

Jones hummed in acknowledgment, his skepticism fading like footprints on a busy sidewalk. He had seen Carmella interrogate with tact, navigate through emotional patrons with ease, unravel threads of the tight-knit community's fabric without a snag. Respect bloomed in his chest, a reluctant bud pushing through the soil of doubt.

"Could be a lead," he admitted, scanning the list. "High cost, high risk."

"Exactly," Carmella replied, her gaze sharp. "And with the festival..."

"Someone might've wanted him out of the way," Jones finished the thought, his voice low.

Together, they turned to the office, where Tony's personal effects lay scattered, untouched since the discovery. The air was cold, the silence between them pregnant with possibility. They rifled through papers, drawers, old menus. Each item held potential—a clue, a secret, a motive.

"Detective," Carmella called out suddenly, her hand hovering over an open ledger.

Jones moved to her side, watching as she pointed to a series of figures. "These numbers are off. Way off."

"Embezzlement?" Jones pondered aloud, his brow creasing.

"Or blackmail," Carmella suggested, her mind racing ahead.

"Both give us a motive," Jones agreed, his voice tinged with a newfound admiration for her shrewdness.

"Let's follow the money," Jones decided, his eyes meeting Carmella's.

"Lead the way, Detective," Carmella responded, a slight smile playing on her lips.

Chapter 3

The bell above the door jingled as Carmella pushed into Nonna's Slice of Heaven, her refuge turned crime scene. The aroma of baking dough and simmering tomato sauce wrapped around her like a familiar embrace, but today it did little to calm the flutter in her chest. She scanned the room until her eyes landed on Kathleen, perched at their usual corner booth, her eyes sharp, her auburn hair a fiery banner in the homely pizzeria.

"Hey," Carmella said, sliding into the seat opposite her friend.

"Hey yourself," replied Kathleen, the corners of her mouth lifting in a brief, supportive smile.

Carmella clasped her hands on the table, the wood grain solid under her touch. "We need to find out who killed Tony."

"Agreed." Kathleen leaned forward, elbows resting on the table. "It's time to dig into Tony's life. See who might have wanted him gone."

"His relationships were...complicated." Carmella's voice carried a hint of hesitation, mindful of the man's boisterous spirit now silenced.

"Complicated is what we do best." Kathleen's smile was a sliver of confidence.

"Motives then. We start with motives." Carmella's resolve hardened. She pictured Tony, always in motion, his laughter booming through his own pizzeria, his competitive edge sometimes a sharpened knife.

"Exactly." Kathleen nodded. "Who stood to gain from Tony's absence? Who felt threatened by his success?"

"Or maybe someone from his past?" Carmella suggested, tapping a finger against the tabletop.

"Could be." Kathleen's gaze was calculating, already sifting through Ideas.

"Then we sift through every slice of his life," Carmella declared, the metaphor fitting amidst the scent of marinara and mozzarella.

"Let's cut through the crust," Kathleen agreed.

Together, they rose from the booth, two friends united against an unseen enemy, ready to piece together a puzzle left in the wake of tragedy.

Carmella strode to the door, the bell chiming above her as she pushed it open. She paused, glancing back at Kathleen who was sliding out of the booth, her movements fluid and purposeful.

"Tony's place," Carmella said, squinting against the afternoon sun that spilled onto the sidewalk. "His staff might know more than they realize."

"Good call." Kathleen fell into step beside her, a breeze teasing strands of hair across her face. "Employees see everything, hear everything."

They walked in silence, the rhythmic tap of their shoes on the pavement marking time. The pizzeria loomed ahead, its windows dark, the neon 'Open' sign unlit—a slumbering giant holding secrets.

"Once we're done there," Kathleen suggested, her tone even but insistent, "the library should be our next stop."

"Library?" Carmella's eyebrows lifted.

"Articles, archives, anything on Tony's past disputes." Kathleen's stride never wavered. "If he stepped on toes, those toes would leave a print."

"Smart." Carmella nodded, already seeing Kathleen amidst stacks of dusty books and old newspapers, piecing together stories hidden within the pages.

"Plus," Kathleen added with a smirk, "I have my ways with the librarian."

"Perks of the trade?" Carmella quipped.

"Exactly." Kathleen winked.

The bell above the door chimed its greeting as Carmella pushed into Tony's pizzeria, Kathleen a shadow at her side. The scent of tomato and oregano hung heavy in the air, a ghost of meals past. They paused, scanning the room where chairs perched atop tables like weary birds. A single employee, mop in hand, turned at their entrance, eyebrows knitted in curiosity.

"Hi there," Carmella began, her voice a blend of warmth and compassion. "We're hoping to ask a few questions about Tony."

"Sure." The employee leaned on his mop, eyes tracing the empty space where Tony once stood. "What do you wanna know?"

"Any unusual comings and goings before...before it happened?" Kathleen tilted her head, her tone light, inviting trust.

He shrugged. "Tony had his regulars, his routines. Nothing weird, except..."

"Except?" Carmella leaned in, encouraging.

"Otto Marks was around more than usual," he said, lowering his voice. "They didn't get along. Everyone knew that."

"Otto Marks?" Kathleen's lips pursed.

"Runs the pizza place across town. They were always at each other's throats over who made the best pie." He snorted. "Seems stupid now, doesn't it?"

"Did you notice anything specific? Any arguments or threats?" Carmella asked, her gaze steady.

"Last week, they had words. Otto was bragging about some new recipe, waving it in Tony's face. Tony told him to shove it." The employee's shoulders rose and fell. "That's all I got."

"Thank you," Kathleen said, her smile tight. "You've been very helpful."

The pair stepped out into the daylight, the door's chime a soft farewell. They shared a look, the same thought flickering between them.

"Otto Marks," whispered Carmella, decision hardening her features. "We need to dig deeper."

"Absolutely," Kathleen murmured, her eyes gleaming with the thrill of the hunt. "Let's see what Mr. Marks has been cooking up besides pizza."

The scent of aged paper and lemon polish greeted Carmella and Kathleen as they entered the library. Kathleen's fingers danced across the computer keyboard as she scanned the screen with practiced ease. Carmella paced behind her, the click of her shoes a staccato against the hush.

"Here," Kathleen said, pulling up articles from the local newspaper archives. "Otto Marks. There's a lot to sift through."

"Start from the beginning?" Carmella suggested, leaning over Kathleen's shoulder.

"Way back," Kathleen affirmed, clicking on an article dated seven years prior. It detailed how Otto's pizzeria had risen in popularity, eclipsing others in town. A photo showed Otto, triumphant, holding a trophy at a local bake-off.

"Keep going," Carmella urged, her voice low.

Kathleen scrolled, finding more articles, interviews where Otto spoke of his 'unique methods' and 'unmatched quality'. The language was guarded, but the subtext clear—Otto played for keeps.

"Here." Kathleen pointed at the screen. "Complaints filed against him. Allegations of sabotage."

"Any proof?" Carmella asked, her brow furrowing.

"Settled out of court," Kathleen whispered. "Quietly."

"Typical," Carmella muttered. Her mind painted a picture of Otto, lurking in the shadows, orchestrating the fall of his competitors. She could almost hear his calculated words, see the cold eyes assessing, planning.

"Look at this." Kathleen tapped on another link. "A pattern of intimidation. Suppliers pressured to choose sides. Rivalries no one wants to talk about."

"Tony wouldn't have backed down from that," Carmella said, a note of respect threading her voice.

"Exactly." Kathleen leaned back. "Tony was a threat to Otto's empire."

"An empire built on fear," Carmella concluded, a bitter taste in her mouth.

"Let's print everything we have," Kathleen decided, her tone resolute.

Carmella nodded, her determination solidifying like concrete. They would peel back the layers of Otto's past, expose every dirty secret. For Tony. For justice.

Carmella's finger hovered over the mouse, her pulse quickening as she clicked through the digital archives. The printer beside them whirred to life, churning out page after page of Otto's veiled threats and underhanded dealings. She could almost smell the ink staining his reputation with every printed word.

"Here," Kathleen said, breaking the silence. Her voice was a sharp contrast to the rhythmic hum of the library. "See this? Tony's last interview before he... you know."

She pointed at the glowing screen. Carmella leaned in, scanning the text. Tony had spoken of plans for expansion, new recipes that would 'revolutionize' the local pizza scene. His confidence leapt from the page, a clear challenge to any who doubted him.

"Otto must have seen this," Carmella whispered.

"Must have hated it," Kathleen added, her lips tight.

The two friends exchanged a look, a silent acknowledgment of the gravity of their discovery. Tony's ambition had been a beacon, one that shone too brightly for Otto's liking. A beacon he had sought to snuff out.

"His motive," Carmella murmured.

"Clear as day," Kathleen confirmed.

They gathered the printed pages, stacking them into a neat pile. Each sheet was a piece of the puzzle, each line a potential lead.

"We can't let Otto get away with this," Carmella said, her hands clenching the papers slightly.

Kathleen nodded. "We'll need to confront him. Show him we know what he's done."

"Right." Carmella stood, her resolve steeling. "But carefully. We can't tip him off."

"I know." Kathleen rose, her height commanding. "We gather everything, then we hit him with the truth."

"Let's hope it's enough," Carmella sighed. They both knew that Otto wouldn't go down without a fight.

"Enough for what?" Kathleen asked, a wry edge to her question.

"Enough to lock him up," Carmella answered, firm.

"Then let's do this," Kathleen said, her tone echoing Carmella's.

The two women left the library, evidence in hand, ready to face the man who had turned Wavecrest Cove's pizza scene into a battleground. They would confront Otto Marks, armed with facts.

Sunlight streamed through the blinds of Nonna's Slice of Heaven, casting stripes of light and shadow across the checkered tablecloth. Carmella Moretti sat with her back straight, eyes intent on Kathleen, who was shuffling through stacks of printouts and handwritten notes. The aroma of tomato sauce and fresh dough lingered in the air, a comforting backdrop to the tense atmosphere.

"Best Pizzeria Bake-off Festival," Carmella said, breaking the silence. "Otto will be there, basking in the glory he thinks he's earned."

Kathleen nodded, her eyes sharp like cut glass. "Public. Risky. But it might just work."

Carmella reached for a pen, tapping it against the tabletop. "We need to be precise, Kath. One shot at exposing him."

"Timing is everything." Kathleen leaned in, her voice a whisper. "We do it after the judges' decision, before the winner's announced. Maximum impact."

"Okay."

They stood, gathering their materials. Carmella folded the evidence neatly, tucking it inside a folder. Her movements were deliberate, each fold a crease in Otto's fabricated world.

"Let's pack this up," Kathleen said, gathering the remaining pages. "We'll go over everything once more at my place."

"Good plan."

The walk to Kathleen's house was silent, save for the crunch of autumn leaves beneath their feet. Once inside, they spread out their ammunition on the dining room table: newspaper clippings, bank statements, witness statements. Each item sang the same tune—a song of greed and desperation.

"Imagine, Otto Marks, undone by his own hubris," Kathleen mused, a half-smile playing on her lips.

"Justice has a funny way of catching up," Carmella replied, her tone even, but her hands betrayed a slight tremor.

They worked into the evening, the sky outside darkening to a velvety blue. Their preparations were meticulous, every question anticipated, every response rehearsed. They would leave nothing to chance.

"Are you ready for tomorrow?" Kathleen asked, her expression unreadable.

"Ready as I'll ever be," Carmella answered, her heart pounding a fierce rhythm. "Tony deserves this much."

"Then let's bring down a kingpin." Kathleen's gaze met Carmella's, a silent pact forged between them.

"See you at dawn," Carmella said, clutching the folder to her chest as she stepped out into the night. The crisp air filled her lungs, sharpening her senses.

Mama Mia It's Murder

Tomorrow, Wavecrest Cove would watch as truth sliced through deceit, as clear as the edge of a well-honed pizza cutter. Tomorrow, they would confront Otto Marks.

The scent of baking dough and simmering tomato sauce wafted through the air as Carmella and Kathleen stepped into the bustling festival. A cacophony of laughter, chatter, and the occasional sizzle from a cooking station filled the autumn afternoon. Brightly colored booths adorned with checkered tablecloths lined the streets of Wavecrest Cove, each vying for attention with their array of pizzas and Italian delicacies.

Carmella's gaze swept the crowd, her eyes sharp, picking out faces and movements with an advertiser's keen sense of observation. Beside her, Kathleen's posture was relaxed, but her mind worked like the catalog system she knew so well, categorizing and discarding irrelevant details in search of their quarry.

"Remember, casual," Kathleen murmured, her tone light but carrying an undercurrent of steel.

"Of course," Carmella replied, her voice steady. The petite woman moved with purpose, her brown hair bouncing slightly with each step.

They wove through groups of families and clusters of teenagers, past children with cheeks smeared with marinara. The aroma of garlic and oregano surrounded them, a familiar comfort that under any other circumstance would have elicited fond memories of Nonna's kitchen.

Ahead, near a booth crowned with a banner proclaiming 'Marks' Marvelous Margheritas,' stood Otto. He was a still point amidst the motion, his lean figure erect as he surveyed his domain. Short graying hair gave him a distinguished air, though his eyes calculating, missed nothing.

"Showtime," Kathleen said, her sight locking onto their target.

"Let's do this," Carmella agreed, feeling the weight of the evidence folder against her side.

They edged closer to Otto's booth, slipping between patrons with plates piled high, their approach unnoticed by the pizzeria owner engaged in conversation. Otto's voice, quiet yet commanding, drifted over to them as they closed the distance.

"Quality above all," they heard him say, adjusting his glasses with a precise gesture. "That's what sets us apart."

"Indeed, it does," Carmella said, stepping into Otto's line of sight, her presence drawing a pause in the conversations around them. Kathleen remained a silent sentinel at her side, her expression unreadable yet undeniably intense.

Otto looked at them, his expression one of mild surprise that quickly shifted to a guarded neutrality. "Ms. Moretti, Ms. Murray," he greeted, inclining his head slightly. "To what do I owe the pleasure?"

"Let's just say we're interested in your recipe for success," Carmella stated, her tone deceptively light, her eyes locked on Otto's, searching for any flicker of weakness.

The festival air buzzed with the aroma of baking dough and melting cheese. Carmella's hand tightened on the folder, a shield of truth in a sea of unsuspecting revelers. Otto's booth loomed ahead, festooned with ribbons that fluttered like the heartbeat racing in her chest.

"Are you ready?" whispered Kathleen, her gaze fixed on their quarry.

"Ready as I'll ever be," Carmella replied, throat dry.

They sidestepped a laughing family, their cheer a stark contrast to the gravity of the task at hand. Otto's back was to them now, his posture rigid with pride. His voice, usually so controlled, rose with passion as he expounded on the superiority of his ingredients.

"Mr. Marks," Carmella called out, stepping forward. The murmur of the crowd hushed, sensing the undercurrent of confrontation.

Otto turned, surprise flickering over his features before settling into a mask of calm. "Ms. Moretti," he said, voice smooth but eyes wary.

"We've been looking into Tony Bianco's... unfortunate departure," Kathleen interjected, her words crisp and pointed.

"Oh?" Otto tilted his head, curiosity etched into the lines of his face, betraying nothing else.

"His departure," Carmella echoed, stressing the word, "which seems to benefit you greatly."

A collective intake of breath rippled through the onlookers. Otto's lips thinned, the only sign of his composure cracking.

"Accusations require proof," he retorted, his tone steady.

"Which we have," Carmella said, pulling the folder open to reveal documents bathed in the golden afternoon light. Otto's eyes darted down, then up, meeting Carmella's steady gaze.

"Tony's murder deserves justice," she declared, her voice carrying across the silent throng. Otto swallowed, the act visible and telling.

"Let's see what you've found," he conceded, steel in his voice, masking the tremor of defeat.

Carmella and Kathleen exchanged a glance, united in purpose. This was it—the moment of truth.

Patti Petrone Miller

Chapter 4

Carmella Moretti pushed open the door to Frankie's Pizza Haven, her petite frame eclipsed by the doorway's broad shadow. The scent of tomato sauce and melting cheese enveloped her as she stepped inside, warmth from the ovens warding off the evening chill. Kathleen followed close behind, her red hair catching the light like strands of polished copper.

The pizzeria teemed with life. Families huddled over checkered tablecloths, laughter mingling with the clinking of cutlery. A child waved a slice of pepperoni pizza, his cheeks smeared with sauce.

"Smells like heaven," Kathleen remarked, her eyes gleaming with mischief.

"Feels like home," Carmella replied, her gaze sweeping over the scene.

Behind the counter, Frankie Marino commandeered his domain. His hands worked the dough with practiced ease, fingers pressing and turning with a rhythm born of years in the kitchen. Dark curls escaped from beneath his chef's hat, framing a face alight with focus.

"Excuse me, Frankie?" Carmella called out, her voice threading through the din.

Frankie looked up, a smile crinkling the corners of his eyes. "Ciao! What can I do for you, signorine?"

"Hi, I'm Carmella Moretti," she said, extending a hand that was quickly enveloped by Frankie's flour-dusted grip. "And this is my friend, Kathleen."

"Moretti... any relation to Nonna's Slice of Heaven?" he asked, recognition sparking.

"That's right," she confirmed. "I'm her granddaughter."

"Ah, che peccato about your nonna's place," Frankie lamented, wiping his hands on an apron streaked with the day's work.

"Actually, we're here because of Tony Bianco," Carmella continued, her voice steady despite the flutter in her stomach. "We think you might be able to help us solve his murder."

"Tony?" Frankie's brow furrowed, the joviality fading into concern. "That's a serious accusation. What makes you think I can help?"

"Because," Carmella said, locking eyes with him, "you know this town's secrets, especially the ones baked into its pizza crusts."

Frankie's gaze held Carmella's, the flicker of intrigue evident in his widening eyes. Dough took shape beneath his touch, his palms pressing a perfect circle onto the floured surface with a deftness that spoke of countless hours at the craft. The ambient noise of conversations and cutlery clinking against plates filled the space around them, yet in this moment, it seemed to fade into the background.

"Murder, you say?" Frankie's voice carried a note of curiosity over the sizzle of pies in the oven.

"Si," Carmella replied, her own hands nervously twisting the strap of her purse. "And we think you could hold the missing piece."

"Tony was a good man," Frankie murmured, a hint of sadness lacing his words. His dough now lay flat, set aside with a reverence for the task interrupted.

"Follow me." He gestured, wiping his hands on his apron once more before navigating through the maze of tables. Customers continued their meals, oblivious to the gravity of the conversation about to unfold.

Carmella and Kathleen trailed behind Frankie, their footsteps in sync with each other's, the clack of Kathleen's heels punctuating their movement. They arrived at a corner booth, nestled away from the heart of the pizzeria's hustle. Here, the clamor softened to a gentle hum, the aroma of basil and tomato more pronounced.

"Parlate," Frankie said, sliding into the seat opposite them, an invitation to speak in his simple command.

Carmella leaned forward, the urgency clear in her posture. "We need your insight, Frankie. About the rivalries, the secrets... anything that might point us in the right direction."

"Everything has its place," he began, hands coming together as if to mold his thoughts like the dough he so masterfully shaped. "Just like ingredients on a pizza. I will help you find the right combination."

"Thank you, Frankie," Kathleen chimed in, her smile a mix of relief and gratitude.

"Let's start from the beginning, then," Frankie proposed, his tone firm yet open, a mentor ready to guide his protégés through uncharted territory.

Carmella perched on the edge of her seat, a ripple of anticipation coursing through her. She glanced at Kathleen, who mirrored her eager posture. The clink of cutlery and murmur of conversation faded into the background as they fixed their eyes on Frankie.

"Okay," Frankie said, clasping his hands on the table, "where to start?" His gaze flitted between Carmella and Kathleen, a spark of enthusiasm igniting in his deep-set eyes.

"Ever since I was a ragazzo, pizza has been my world," he began, leaning back as though his heart brimmed with the tales he was about to share. "But it's not just about the dough and the sauce. It's a dance, a competition, an art."

Carmella nodded, hanging on his every word. What could be more important than the perfect crust?

"Back in Napoli," Frankie continued, a wistful tone creeping into his voice, "I went head-to-head with some of the best pizzaioli. Once, during La Festa della Pizza, eh?" He chuckled, a rich, resonant sound. "We had this massive throw down. Imagine, hundreds of us, flames leaping from the ovens, the air thick with the scent of melting mozzarella."

Kathleen leaned in with interest. "And the rivalries?"

"Ah, sì," Frankie said, gesturing expansively. "There was Gino—" He paused, his smile turning sly. "Gino thought he had the upper hand with his secret tomato blend."

Carmella's breath hitched. A secret blend? Could that be a clue?

"But," Frankie added, lowering his voice, "what matters is not just what you put on your pizza, but how you make it sing. That's where the true magic lies."

The warmth from the oven nearby seemed to echo his sentiment, wrapping around Carmella like a comforting embrace. She felt a stirring within, a desire to uncover the secrets of the craft and, perhaps, the mystery that brought her here.

Frankie's hands carved the air as he spoke, shaping invisible pies with a flourish that left Carmella and Kathleen rapt. "In Wavecrest Cove," he said, "the dough flies thicker than the fog on the bay."

"Every tomato, every basil leaf—it's a declaration of war." His fingers mimicked the delicate sprinkling of herbs, a maestro conducting an orchestra of flavors.

Carmella's mind raced. The rivalries ran deep, deeper than she'd imagined. Frankie's tales were windows into a world where every pizza was a battleground, every topping a tactic.

"Luca down at The Rolling Pin," Frankie confided, lowering his voice to a conspiratorial whisper, "he prides himself on his wild yeast." He shook his head, eyes twinkling. "But it's not just about the fermentation—it's the heart you knead into the bread."

Kathleen's laughter bubbled up, quick and light. "And what about Nonna's?" she asked. "What's our secret weapon?"

Frankie leaned back, appraising Carmella with a knowing look. "Passion," he said simply. "You've got to love the pie more than the competition."

A resolve settled over Carmella. She would learn, she would bake, she would love—every pie a testament to her grandfather's legacy. She'd make Nonna's Slice of Heaven sing again, one perfect crust at a time.

Frankie caught the spark in Carmella's eyes, the flicker of fierce determination. "Venite," he beckoned, a grin spreading across his face as he motioned her towards the sacred space behind the counter—a stage for the pizzaiolo's performance. With a flourish, he dusted flour across the wooden countertop, a blank canvas awaiting its masterpiece.

"Watch closely," he instructed, as Carmella leaned in, her senses tuned to his every movement. He took a ball of dough, one that had risen just right, and began to work it with hands that knew only the language of creation. Under Frankie's touch, the dough stretched, yielding yet resilient. His fingers danced, palms pressing and pulling, transforming the pliable mass into something larger, something promising.

"Like this," Frankie said, lifting the burgeoning disk with a practiced spin. The dough obeyed, twirling in mid-air, gravity an accomplice in its artful expansion. Carmella's breath hitched, witnessing the alchemy of motion and skill.

"Balance and momentum," he murmured, catching the dough with a gentle caress. It landed back on the countertop, no longer just dough but a thin, even crust, the foundation of what would soon be a testament to tradition and innovation alike.

Carmella's gaze followed the contours of the crust, the edges just right, the center invitingly soft. She imagined her own hands, her own pies spinning to life, each one a step closer to fulfilling the promise she'd made herself, to her grandfather, to Nonna's Slice of Heaven.

"Your turn will come," Frankie assured her, his smile an echo of the confidence swelling within her. "Perfection is patience."

The aroma of yeast and flour mingled in the air, a scent that spoke of homecomings and new beginnings. Carmella watched, committed to memory the way Frankie moved, the way the dough seemed to listen to him. She would learn, and she would succeed. This was her craft now, too.

Carmella's hands trembled as she scooped up the round of dough. The soft mass felt alive, full of potential and secrets she was eager to unlock. Frankie stood beside her, a tower of confidence in his flour-dusted apron.

"Keep it airy," he instructed, his voice a steady hum over the din of the pizzeria. "Let it breathe."

She mimicked his earlier motions, palms pressing and stretching, but the dough fought back, springing into its former shape with stubborn elasticity. Carmella frowned, her fingers fumbling for the rhythm that had seemed so effortless in Frankie's hands.

"Ah, don't be shy," Frankie chuckled, stepping closer. His hands hovered over hers, not touching, just guiding. "Dance with it, Carmella. It's a partner, not an opponent."

Encouraged, Carmella gave the dough another whirl. Her toss was clumsy, the disk lopsided as it returned to her waiting palms. A ripple of frustration passed through her, but she swallowed it down, replaced by the resolve that had brought her this far from the city.

"Brava, you're getting there!" Frankie's praise was genuine. He adjusted her grip subtly. "Fingers like this, see? Gentle, yet firm."

She nodded, tried again. The dough soared, a timid spin, but better. It landed askew on the countertop, a testament to progress, not perfection.

"See, every try brings you closer," Frankie said, his belief as warm as the oven's glow. "You'll charm the stubbornness out of any dough."

Carmella's smile returned, her heart syncing with the pulse of the kitchen. She balled the dough once more, ready for another round, ready to prove him right.

Carmella's hands moved with newfound purpose, the dough yielding to her touch as if recognizing its master. She stretched it, her movements more assured now, the rhythm natural and fluid. The scent of yeast and flour filled her senses, grounding her in the moment.

"Good, good," Frankie nodded, his eyes following her progress. "You're feeling it, si?"

She looked up, met his approving gaze. "I think I am."

"Let's see the toss, then," he encouraged, stepping back to give her space.

She lifted the dough, felt its weight balanced between her fingers. A breath, a flick of the wrists, and it spun upward, catching the light of the overhead lamps. It descended like a slow-motion dream, more symmetrical this time, and she caught it cleanly.

"Perfetto!" Frankie clapped his hands once, the sound sharp in the busy pizzeria.

Heat flushed Carmella's cheeks—not from the ovens, but pride. She grinned, the dough obedient beneath her palms.

"Nonna's Slice of Heaven," she murmured to herself, the words a promise on her lips.

"Will be better than ever," Frankie finished for her, reading her thoughts. His smile was a shared secret, a bond over dough and dreams.

"Thanks to you," Carmella said, placing the dough on the peel with care.

"Ah, I just gave a little nudge." Frankie waved a dismissive hand. "You have the heart of a true pizzaiola."

As the oven's warmth enveloped them, Carmella's confidence bloomed like yeast in sugar. Her future, once clouded by doubt, now stretched before her, as open and full of possibility as the evening sky outside Frankie's Pizza Haven.

Chapter 5

The sky blushed with the first light of dawn as Carmella turned the key in the lock of Nonna's Slice of Heaven. Her fingers were steady, betraying none of the storm that brewed within her -- a tempest of determination to wash away the stain of suspicion from her name. The door creaked open, its old hinges singing a familiar tune of welcome that seemed out of place with the tension that clung to Carmella like the morning mist.

She stepped over the threshold and flicked on the lights. The pizzeria sprang to life; ovens yawned awake, ready to cradle dough into golden crusts. A glance through the window revealed the gathering crowd. Their whispers fluttered into the early morning air, a flock of curious birds peering and prying from their perch on the sidewalk.

"Early risers or something else?" she muttered to herself.

Carmella adjusted the collar of her apron, her fingers brushing against fabric as if to smooth out the worries etched in her mind. With each onlooker's gaze that met her eyes, she felt a prickling sensation, like the first sizzle of onions hitting hot oil.

"Morning, folks," she called out, her voice cutting through the low hum of speculation. She offered a smile, warm yet lined with an unspoken challenge. Her petite frame leaned against the doorframe, a lighthouse standing firm against the tide of doubt.

"Fresh batch of Sicilian coming up. Who's hungry?" Her words hung in the air, an invitation laced with the aroma of tomato and basil that began to waft from within the pizzeria.

Carmella inhaled deeply, her chest rising with the weight of her plan to action. She crossed the pizzeria's threshold and stood before the assembled crowd. The morning chill kissed her cheeks, a stark contrast to the warmth she summoned from within.

"Good morning," she said, her voice steady as she met their gazes one by one. "I'm Carmella Moretti, and this," she gestured behind her to the cozy eatery, "is my grandfather's legacy."

A murmur rippled through the onlookers, feet shuffling, eyes searching for the truth beneath her words.

"Nonna's Slice of Heaven isn't just a business. It's a piece of community history," she continued, her hands unconsciously clasping together, fingers intertwined in silent strength. "And I'm here to make sure it remains a place where memories are baked into every slice."

The scent of fresh dough and simmering sauce began to mingle with the salty sea air. Carmella's expression softened, inviting trust.

"I've come back to Wavecrest Cove to honor that tradition," she said. "To serve you with the same dedication my Nonno did." Her eyes glinted with the sincerity of her pledge. "I am committed to this town, to this pizzeria, and to clearing my name."

Her words hung between them, an offering of honesty and hope.

"Please, step inside," Carmella beckoned, gesturing toward the open door where the aroma of baking pizza promised comfort and warmth. "Let Nonna's Slice of Heaven enchant your senses."

The first hesitant steps echoed on the tiled floor as townsfolk crossed the threshold. Inside, golden light washed over varnished wood and gleaming countertops. The clink of cutlery and the sizzle from the kitchen filled the space with the music of a morning in motion.

"Welcome," she greeted each newcomer with a smile. "I'm glad you're here."

"Smells like my childhood," an elderly gentleman murmured, his skepticism faltering under the spell of nostalgia.

"Mine too," Carmella replied, her voice tinged with pride. "The recipe is unchanged."

She moved among the guests, her presence a calm anchor as they drifted in a sea of curiosity and hunger. Her hands moved with practiced grace, setting down napkins, straightening chairs, all the while maintaining a steady stream of conversation.

"Fresh basil from the garden," she pointed to the green plants basking in the window light. "It's the secret touch."

"Feels like home," a woman said, her voice softening as she took in the familiar checkered tablecloths and framed photos on the walls.

"Exactly what I hoped for," Carmella's response was heartfelt, her mission clear. She had opened more than just the doors this morning; she had opened a dialogue, a possibility for connection and understanding.

"Try the corner booth," she suggested to a family with young children. "Best view of the harbor."

"Thank you, Carmella," the mother said, recognition blooming in her tone.

Carmella's smile didn't waver as she watched them settle in, their initial wariness dissolving like yeast into dough. She had planted seeds of trust, and with care, they would rise.

Carmella navigated the pizzeria with ease, her senses attuned to the subtle shifts in mood. A furrowed brow here, a hesitant glance there; she caught each sign like a seasoned sailor reading the wind. She approached a clustered group of regulars, their hushed tones breaking as they noticed her.

"Morning," she began, "I know you've got questions."

"Is it true what they say about Tony?" one asked, his voice low but tinged with concern.

"Tony and I were competitors, yes, but nothing more." Carmella's words flowed evenly, no hint of evasion. "His passing was a shock to us all."

The man nodded, the tension in his shoulders easing as Carmella's sincerity settled over him. Another woman chimed in, her words laced with worry, "But how can we be sure?"

"Because I loved this town just as he did, and I'm here to prove it," Carmella replied, her gaze steady.

Amidst the murmur of conversations and the clinking of cutlery, Carmella turned toward the kitchen. The aroma of baking dough and melting cheese wafted out as she emerged with a tray of steaming slices, the golden crusts glistening under the warm lights.

"Please, help yourselves," she invited, setting the tray down on the counter.

Eyes lit up, stomachs rumbled in response. Skeptics and supporters alike edged closer, drawn by the universal language of good food. As bites were taken, expressions softened. Nods of approval were exchanged over mouthfuls of gooey mozzarella and tangy tomato sauce.

"Grandpa's recipe never disappoints," Carmella said, watching faces brighten at the taste.

"Delicious," a gruff voice admitted, the word slicing through years of culinary rivalry.

"Thank you." Carmella's smile was genuine, her relief palpable. "There's more where that came from."

One by one, barriers crumbled, replaced by the shared experience of Nonna's culinary embrace. Each slice served was a silent testament to Carmella's devotion to her craft, and to Wavecrest Cove. And bite by bite, the tide began to turn in her favor.

Carmella navigated through the bustling pizzeria with practiced ease, her senses attuned to each customer's mood. The clatter of dishes mixed with the low hum of satisfied chatter. Amidst the warmth of the ovens and the rustic charm of checkered tablecloths, her eyes locked onto a solitary figure: Sarah, the local food blogger, known for her incisive reviews and sharp tongue.

A furrow creased Sarah's brow as she scrutinized the scene, her pen poised above a notepad like a scepter of judgment. Carmella exhaled softly and made her way over, wiping her flour-dusted hands on her apron.

"Sarah, isn't it?" Carmella greeted, her voice steady despite the flutter in her chest.

"Carmella Moretti," Sarah acknowledged, her gaze cool and assessing.

"Mind if I sit?" Carmella gestured to the empty chair across from Sarah, who nodded, her expression unreadable.

"Your thoughts?" Carmella ventured, folding her hands on the table.

Sarah tapped her pen against the notepad. "Curious place. Curious times," she said, her words measured.

"Curious is one word for it," Carmella replied with a wry smile that didn't quite reach her eyes. She leaned forward, her resolve clear in her steady gaze. "I'm here to keep my grandpa's dream alive, Sarah. And I need you to believe me when I say I had no part in Tony's death."

Sarah studied Carmella, the scrutiny unrelenting. "It's what they all claim, isn't it?"

"Maybe." Carmella's shoulders squared. "But I'm different. I want the truth just as much as anyone else here—more, even."

"Because it'll clear your name?" Sarah's voice was flat, her pen still now.

"Because it's right," Carmella countered, her sincerity unfeigned. "Tony and I may have been rivals in business, but his loss... it's a loss for all of Wavecrest Cove."

"Ah." Sarah's lips curved, not quite a smile. "The bigger picture."

"Exactly." Carmella nodded. "And until we find out who's responsible, none of us can truly move forward."

"An admirable stance," Sarah conceded, her posture relaxing incrementally.

"Admirable and true," Carmella affirmed. "So, what do you say, Sarah? Will you give Nonna's Slice of Heaven a fair shot?"

Sarah paused, pen hovering once more. Then, slowly, she placed it down, her features softening ever so slightly. "I'll write what I see, Carmella. And what I taste."

"Then let's make sure you see and taste the best we've got." Carmella stood, her smile genuine this time. "Starting with another slice —or two—on the house."

As Carmella returned to the kitchen, the buzz of conversation behind her, she allowed herself a small moment of hope. One heart at a time, she thought. That's how trust is rebuilt.

Carmella slid a steaming slice of pepperoni pizza onto a ceramic plate, the scent of oregano and melted cheese filling the air. She carried it over to where Sarah sat, observing with an analytical eye. The blogger chewed slowly, thoughtfully, her skepticism melting away bite by bite.

"Flavors are spot on," Sarah murmured, jotting down notes. She glanced up at Carmella, a glimmer of respect in her gaze. "You've got skill, I'll give you that."

"Thank you," Carmella replied, tucking a loose strand of hair behind her ear. "I hope you feel the passion that goes into every pie."

Sarah's pen paused on the paper. She locked eyes with Carmella, searching for the hint of a sales pitch. Instead, she found earnestness, an open book pleading to be read fairly. "Alright, Carmella Moretti. You've got my attention—and a chance. My review will tell it like it is." Her voice softened, almost imperceptibly. "No bias."

"Fair is all I'm asking for." Carmella's smile reached her eyes.

The exchange was brief, but potent. Sarah's words, once released into the heart of Wavecrest Cove, rippled through the town like a stone skipped across the bay. Conversations sparked at the post office, murmurs over coffee at the diner, nods of agreement along the boardwalk.

"Did you hear? Sarah thinks the new girl might be okay."
"Her pizza? It's actually good. Like, really good."
"Maybe we were wrong about Carmella..."

Doubts receded as Nonna's Slice of Heaven's door chimed more frequently. Folks entered with curiosity, left with content smiles and satisfied appetites. The pizzeria hummed with newfound life, its tables hosting old friends and new patrons alike.

"Welcome back!" Carmella greeted each arrival with warmth, remembering names, asking about families. With every handshake, every shared laugh, walls crumbled. Trust sprouted from the fertile ground of community spirit.

"Give her a chance," Sarah's followers echoed. "She's one of us."

And bit by bit, Carmella felt the tide turn.

Sunlight waned, casting a golden hue across Nonna's Slice of Heaven. The tables were full. Laughter and chatter filled the space. Carmella was in the thick of it, apron dusted with flour, hands moving deftly to slide another pizza into the oven. The bell above the door chimed incessantly, announcing new customers — skeptics turned supporters.

"Another Margherita, Carmella?" Mr. Simmons called out, waving an empty plate. His earlier frown had flipped, now all smiles.

"Coming right up!" Her voice sang over the sizzle and pop from the kitchen.

Carmella worked tirelessly, her energy infectious. She tossed dough with practiced ease, ingredients landing with precision. Piping hot slices made their rounds, each bite affirming her place in Wavecrest Cove. The aroma of basil and melted cheese lingered, a promise of comfort, of home.

"Never knew a Moretti could cook like this," Mrs. Henderson admitted, eyes twinkling as she savored a slice.

"Grandpa taught me well," Carmella replied, her pride gentle but evident.

The oven's warmth wasn't just from the fire. The community's embrace kindled something deeper. Every nod of approval, every murmur of surprise at the taste, fueled her resolve. Carmella's dedication, once questioned, now celebrated.

As shadows stretched and the dinner rush ebbed, Carmella took a moment. She leaned against the counter, gaze sweeping over the diners.

They were laughing, sharing stories, building memories within these walls she fought so hard to preserve. Their acceptance was her triumph.

"Good job today, Carmella," Sarah said, pausing by the exit. "You've earned this."

"Thanks, Sarah." Carmella'ssmile was weary but genuine. "Means the world to me."

Night settled on Wavecrest Cove. Carmella locked up, the click of the key a chorus with her heartbeat. She peered through the window at the empty seats, already imagining them filled come morning. Gratitude swelled within her, mingling with the sense of belonging that had seemed so elusive before.

"Nonna's is going to be okay," she whispered to the darkened pizzeria. With each success, each day closing on a high note, her innocence seemed closer to the surface, ready to break through the lingering doubts like dawn after a long night.

Carmella flipped the sign to "Closed" with a decisive click. The bell above the door jangled softly, a final farewell to the last customer of the day. She stepped back, hands on hips, and surveyed the pizzeria. Crumbs littered the checkered floors, evidence of the day's success.

Her shoes scuffed against the tile as she moved around, picking up stray napkins, realigning salt and pepper shakers. She inhaled deeply, the scent of tomato sauce and baked dough lingering in the air, mingling with the faint tang of cleaning products. A smile tugged at her lips, small but resilient.

She wiped down tables with efficient swipes, the cloth dancing over surfaces in her capable hands. Chairs tucked neatly under each table, order restored. Carmella's heart matched the rhythm of her tasks—steady, hopeful.

"Tomorrow," she murmured, already plotting the specials, the marketing pitch, the personal touch for each regular. Her mind buzzed with strategies, a carryover from her advertising days, now repurposed for her true calling.

The register closed with a satisfying snap. Numbers tallied, hopes quantified. Carmella switched off the lights one by one, shadows reclaiming the space. Outside, the moon cast a silver glow on Wavecrest Cove, turning the streets into ribbons of light and dark.

"Nonna's and I, we're both survivors," she whispered to the stillness. The challenges ahead loomed, unknowns wrapped in opportunity. But tonight, they were distant stars—present, yet unreachable.

    She locked the door behind her, the sound echoing in the quiet street. Alone, yet not lonely, Carmella's steps were measured and sure. Each one a promise, a step toward clearing her name, toward becoming an indelible part of this community that was once her grandfather's dream.

    "Tomorrow," she said again, conviction coloring her voice. The night air wrapped around her like a cloak, cool and comforting. With each breath, she felt her resolve harden, the doubts shed like leaves in autumn. Carmella Moretti would rise with the sun, ready to face whatever lay ahead.

Chapter 6

The bell above the door jangled as Carmella pushed into Tony's pizzeria. The scent of tomato sauce and melted cheese enveloped her, a comforting embrace from the ovens. Kathleen's eyes sparkled with the reflections of the warm, golden light that bathed the dining area, hinting at hidden stories within the walls. Frankie inhaled deeply, his chest rising with an appreciation only a true connoisseur of culinary arts could feel.

"Let's not waste time," Carmella said, glancing around the bustling space. "Tony's killer won't find themselves."

"Agreed," Kathleen replied, tucking a strand of fiery hair behind her ear. She turned to Frankie. "Ready to charm some secrets out of the staff?"

"Always," he grinned, rolling up his sleeves.

They split. Carmella made for the kitchen, dodging between waiters carrying steaming pizzas. Her steps were quick, purposeful. The stainless steel counters gleamed under harsh fluorescent lights. Voices clashed over the sizzle of frying pans.

Kathleen and Frankie moved through the dining area. They navigated between tables where families laughed, couples whispered, and kids reached for another slice. Kathleen's gaze swept across faces, searching for flickers of guilt or fear.

"Let's divide and conquer," she murmured to Frankie.

"Like a pizza," he quipped, heading toward the wood-fired oven where pizzaiolos danced with their peels amongst the flames.

Carmella's gaze locked onto the head chef, Marco, who was vigorously chopping basil, his movements a shade too erratic. The clink of his knife against the cutting board punctuated the hum of the kitchen. She approached, her steps measured.

"Marco," Carmella said, her voice steady. "I need to talk to you about Tony."

The knife stilled. Marco turned, his eyes rimmed red, a sheen of sweat on his brow. "What about him?" he managed, voice barely above a whisper.

"Tony's been murdered." Carmella watched as the words landed like blows. Marco's hand flew to his mouth, his shoulders slumped.

"Murdered? But—" He shook his head, disbelief etching lines into his forehead. "Who would do such a thing?"

"Any recent conflicts catch your attention? Anything unusual?" Carmella kept her tone gentle yet insistent.

Marco hesitated, then nodded. "Last week, there was a heated argument. Tony and one of the suppliers. Over prices, deliveries," he divulged, glancing around to ensure no one else overheard.

"Thanks, Marco. Every detail counts." Carmella offered a comforting touch on his shoulder before backing away.

Across the room, Kathleen leaned against the counter, casual. She caught the eye of a waitress refilling saltshakers.

"Busy night, huh?" Kathleen's smile was easy, inviting conversation.

"Always is." The waitress didn't meet her eyes, focused on her task.

"Everyone in town seems to love this place, even with so much competition," Kathleen prodded, watching closely.

"Tony had a way..." The waitress trailed off, her hands pausing.

"A way?" Kathleen prompted.

"Let's just say, not all the pizzeria owners were fans." A flicker of something crossed the waitress's face—fear? Annoyance?

"Rivalries can be tough," Kathleen sympathized, filing away the reaction. "Tony ever mention anyone specific?"

"Look, I just serve pizzas, not secrets." The waitress resumed her work, a clear end to the conversation.

Kathleen stepped back, her mind whirring with possibilities. She glanced across at Carmella, nodding subtly. They had pieces to puzzle together, leads to follow. And now, a critic to confront.

Frankie sauntered over to the pizza ovens, where a pair of pizzaiolos tossed dough with a rhythm honed by years of practice. The heat from the ovens wrapped around him like an old friend's embrace, and the scent of baking crust and bubbling cheese filled his nostrils.

"Hey, amici," he greeted them with a smile as warm as the glowing embers. "Mind if I watch the masters at work?"

One of the pizzaiolos, a wiry man with flour dusting his apron, shot Frankie a grin. "Only if you're prepared to be dazzled," he joked, spinning the dough expertly on his fingertips.

"Tony taught you his special technique, huh?" Frankie leaned against the counter, his eyes tracking the swift movements of the pizzaiolo's hands.

"Learned from the best," the other pizzaiolo chimed in, sliding a pizza into the roaring oven. "But Tony, he was always pushing the envelope. Trying new things."

"Always looking to outdo the competition?" Frankie probed casually, watching the flames lick the edges of the pizza inside the oven.

"Si, exactly." The first pizzaiolo nodded, his expression tinged with respect. "He wanted to be il migliore."

The conversation flowed, Frankie's innate charm coaxing stories from the pizzaiolos. He listened, absorbing every word.

Across the room, Carmella moved with purpose, her gaze fixed on Tony's office. The door stood ajar, an invitation she couldn't ignore. She slipped inside, the clatter of the dining area fading behind her. The room smelled faintly of ink and pepperoni.

There it was: Tony's desk, cluttered with papers, a testament to the chaos of running a popular pizzeria. Among the mess, a stack of invoices caught her eye. She approached, scanning the top sheet. Her heart thumped—a lead, perhaps?

With a quick glance over her shoulder, Carmella drew out her phone. She captured the stack in a series of photos, the camera's click whisper-soft. Numbers, dates, names—all potential keys to unlock Tony's secrets.

She slipped the phone back into her pocket and turned, ready to rejoin the others. Her mind raced with questions. Who among these pages might want Tony gone? What story did these numbers tell?

Frankie's laughter echoed from the kitchen, a buoyant note amidst the tension. Carmella exhaled slowly, steeling herself. They were piecing together a puzzle—one that led to a murderer hiding in plain sight.

Kathleen leaned casually against the polished counter, her green eyes scanning the room. The din of clinking glasses and laughter wrapped around her, a cocoon of everyday joys and sorrows. Her fingers drummed a silent rhythm on the book she clutched, the only hint of her racing thoughts.

Nearby, two waitstaff whispered, their words slipping through the cracks of conversation. "Did you see Keller's review?" one asked, a wisp of fear in his voice. "Tony was livid."

"Keller's pen is a guillotine," the other replied, trays balancing precariously as he spoke. "Could slice a reputation clean off."

Kathleen's ears perked. Jason Keller. She filed the name next to 'motive' in her mental cabinet.

Across the room, Frankie's smile gleamed in the warm glow of the ovens. He stood among the pizzaiolos, his hands dancing with theirs as they molded dough into future delights. They spoke of Tony, their words a blend of respect and sadness.

"He pushed the craft," one pizzaiolo said, pride lining his weary face. "New recipes. Bold flavors."

"Like what?" Frankie asked, his curiosity a living thing.

"Unusual spices. Exotic cheeses." The pizzaiolo's hands moved with expertise, shaping a tale of culinary adventure.

"Competitors?" Frankie prodded.

"Always," came the reply, a simple truth laid bare.

Frankie nodded, absorbing the ingredients of ambition and rivalry. A new layer to the mystery baked in the heat of the pizza ovens.

Kathleen caught Frankie's eye from across the room and nodded subtly, a signal exchanged. Clues gathered, pieces of a larger puzzle that beckoned them forward into the unknown.

Carmella emerged from the sweltering heat of Tony's kitchen, her phone clutched in hand like a modern-day sleuth's magnifying glass. The air in the dining area felt cooler, dense with whispers and the yeasty promise of pizza. She spotted Kathleen and Frankie huddled together, their heads bowed over a shared secret.

"Got something," Carmella announced, sidling up to them. Her fingers tapped against the screen, bringing up an image of the invoices she'd captured. "Could be big."

Kathleen glanced at the photo, her green eyes narrowing as she pieced together numbers and names. "What are we looking at?"

"Debts," Carmella said crisply, "large orders, unpaid bills. There's a pattern."

Frankie leaned in, his brow furrowed. "Money troubles?" he mused, the Italian lilt in his voice coloring the words.

"More than that," Carmella replied. She recounted Marco's shaken demeanor, the tight-lipped responses of the staff. "Fear's in the air here."

"Keller's review..." Kathleen interjected, the cogs turning behind her sharp gaze. "It was a blow, wasn't it? To Tony's pride, his business."

"His art," Frankie added, gesturing to encapsulate the heart of the pizzeria. "He put himself into those pizzas."

"Exactly." Carmella nodded, a plan forming. "We need to understand the impact. Keller might have more than just ink on his hands."

"Talk to him?" Kathleen asked, the prospect sparking a challenge in her eyes.

"Face to face," Carmella confirmed. They exchanged a look, an unspoken agreement binding them.

"Let's go then," Frankie said, his voice steady, decisive. "Before the trail goes cold."

The trio moved through the pizzeria, past the hum of ovens and low murmur of diners, their steps synchronized in newfound resolve. They pushed out into the day, leaving the cocoon of warmth and the scent of tomato and basil behind. Ahead lay answers, hidden within the scrawl of a critic's pen.

The door closed behind them with a soft jangle, cutting off the warm ambience of Tony's pizzeria. Outside, the chill of the seaside town nipped at their cheeks. Carmella pulled her coat tighter around her, while Kathleen's eyes scanned the street with a detective's precision. Frankie's hands found solace in his pockets, fingers brushing against the slip of paper with the scrawled ingredients for Tony's latest creation.

"Jason Keller won't be expecting us," Carmella said, her voice low but firm.

"Good," Kathleen replied, the corners of her mouth tilting up ever so slightly. "Surprises can loosen tongues."

They moved through the cobbled streets, the quaint shops casting welcoming glows against the encroaching dusk. The scent of salt from the sea melded with lingering traces of garlic and yeast. Waves crashed in the distance, an auditory backdrop to their silent contemplation.

"Keller's review was vicious," Frankie noted, breaking the hush that had settled over them. "Could've pushed Tony over the edge."

"Or someone else," Carmella countered, her mind racing with the possibilities those invoices had suggested.

"Either way," Kathleen interjected, "we find out what Keller knows, what he saw."

Their pace quickened as they approached the heart of Wavecrest Cove, where the critic's office perched like a watchful seagull overlooking the bay. The faint glow of a desk lamp told them Keller was still there, likely poring over his next piece of culinary character assassination.

"Ready?" Carmella asked, her hand on the doorknob to Keller's building.

"Always," Kathleen responded, a spark of excitement in her tone.

"Let's solve this," Frankie added, the weight of Tony's legacy in his voice.

They entered the building, the sea's song fading behind them, replaced by the creak of old floorboards as they ascended the stairs to Jason Keller's office. The truth awaited, shrouded in shadows and whispers, but they were ready to drag it into the light.

Chapter 7

The lock yielded with a click, and the door creaked open. Carmella, Kathleen, and Frankie slipped into Tony's house like shadows chased by the setting sun. Dust motes danced in the slanting light. The scent of lemon polish lingered, a stark contrast to the chaos of the crime committed within these walls.

"Be careful," whispered Carmella, her eyes scanning the dim interior. Her fingers tightened around the strap of her bag—a lifeline in the sea of uncertainty.

Kathleen nodded, her gaze sharp and analytical. "Every detail could be a piece of the puzzle."

Frankie's jaw set. "Let's find what we need." His voice was low, a thread of his usual warmth twisted with tension.

They parted ways, silent as ghosts. Carmella tread lightly toward the kitchen, her senses alert. The room was untouched since the investigation—pots still on the stove, herbs chopped on the cutting board. She looked for anything out of place.

Kathleen floated into the living room, where bookshelves lined the walls. Her fingertips grazed the spines, searching for secrets between the lines. She moved with precision, eyes flickering from one object to another, cataloging everything.

Footsteps thudded softly as Frankie ascended the staircase. The office awaited, a sanctum of personal effects and work documents. He paused at the threshold, taking a steadying breath before stepping over. The room felt charged, as though the air held whispers of heated conversations and late-night musings.

"Anything?" called Carmella from below, her voice barely above a murmur.

"Still looking," Kathleen responded, attention never wavering from her task.

"Same here," came Frankie's reply from upstairs.

Their search continued, the house revealing its secrets one whisper at a time.

Carmella crouched, her fingers tracing the edges of the loose floorboard. A subtle give, a breath held—then a careful pry. The board lifted, cool air escaping from the dark gap below. Her heart drummed against her ribs as she peered into the hidden compartment, the beam of her flashlight cutting through shadows.

"Found something," she whispered, half to herself.

Kathleen paused, her attention caught by the heavy desk dominating the living room. Ornate, ancient, it stood like a silent guardian of Tony's most private thoughts. She pulled at drawers—each one opened but one. Locked. Resolute, she scanned the vicinity—a vase, nondescript, perched innocently on a shelf. Her intuition flared. She reached inside, fingers closing around a small metal key, cool and promising.

"Got it," Kathleen breathed out, satisfaction lacing her tone.

The key slid into the lock with a soft click, a turn, and the drawer gave way. Inside, photographs lay in silent accusation, their glossy surfaces reflecting back a stark reality. Kathleen's gaze sharpened as she sifted through the images, each snapshot a potential lead, a moment captured in time.

"Anything upstairs?" Carmella called, her voice steady despite the adrenaline coursing through her veins.

"Checking," Frankie's distant reply filtered down.

"Let's see what we've got," Carmella said, determination threading through her words.

Kathleen nodded, eyes not leaving the evidence she unearthed. They both knew—their journey into Tony's past was only just beginning.

Frankie's hands moved with practiced ease, flipping through the clutter of papers strewn across Tony's desk. Receipts, order slips, a scribbled recipe for a new marinara sauce—all the detritus of a busy pizzeria owner's life. But Frankie sought the darker ingredients in this mix. The telltale signs of animosity simmering beneath the surface of Wavecrest Cove's culinary camaraderie.

"Anything?" Carmella's voice cut through his concentration.

"Still looking," he murmured, not lifting his gaze.

A drawer resisted his tug, then yielded. Inside, nestled amongst innocuous business correspondence, lay a stack of letters. Envelopes bore the names of familiar eateries, competitors in the relentless dance for dominance. Frankie's pulse quickened; these were no ordinary messages. He drew one out, the paper crisp and foreboding in his grasp.

"Carmella," he called out, "you better see this."

Carmella was on her knees, the contents of the hidden compartment laid bare before her. Her fingers paused as she picked up a letter, unfolding it with care. The light from her flashlight trembled slightly, illuminating words that dripped with hostility. Each sentence, a veiled threat. Each signature, a potential enemy. Tony had been entangled in a web far more treacherous than any of them had imagined.

"Frankie," she said, her voice low, "they're warnings."

"Same here," he replied, standing to join her. "Looks like Tony's been fighting battles on all fronts."

Their eyes met, shared knowledge unspoken between them. The rivalry was more than just a clash of flavors; it was personal, deep-rooted, and now, deadly. They had uncovered the bitterness lurking just beneath the scent of oregano and yeast. It was a taste that promised no sweetness, only the sharp tang of danger.

Kathleen's fingers trembled as she gripped the key, its metal cool and heavy. She slid it into the lock of the vintage desk's drawer, a relic from another time whispering secrets yet to be discovered. With a swift turn, the lock surrendered with an audible click. The drawer slid open, smooth and silent.

She peered inside. A stack of photographs lay in neat order, their glossy surfaces reflecting the dim light. Kathleen picked up the top photo, studying it. It was Tony's pizzeria, the familiar striped awning casting shadows over the entrance. But as she shuffled through the pictures, her gaze fell on other establishments, all competitors. Each snapshot captured storefronts at different angles, under various lighting—dawn's first light, the harsh glare of noon, the subtleties of dusk.

"Guys," Kathleen whispered, holding up the photos for Carmella to see, "Tony was keeping tabs."

Meanwhile, Frankie worked diligently upstairs. His hands, seasoned from years of crafting dough, now navigated the complexities of Tony's cluttered desk. He paused, sensing an anomaly in the wood grain of the paneling. Fingers traced the outline, then pushed. A false front gave way, revealing a hidden space.

"Madre mia," he murmured, eyes widening at the discovery.

Inside rested more photographs. These were not mere storefronts; they were moments frozen in time, each one charged with tension. Frankie pulled them out, one by one. There was Tony, face red, gesturing wildly at a rival owner. Another showed clenched fists, inches from collision. A third caught an index finger jabbing the air, accusations flying like daggers.

"Carmella! Kathleen!" Frankie called out, his voice a mixture of excitement and dread, "You need to see this."

Footsteps echoed as Carmella and Kathleen converged on Frankie's location. They huddled around the photographs spread across Tony's desk. The images spoke volumes, a silent testimony to conflicts that words alone could not convey. Anger. Frustration. Betrayal.

"Look at their expressions," Carmella said, pointing to a particularly heated exchange between Tony and another man whose scowl could curdle milk.

"More than just a pizza war," Frankie added, his tone grave.

Kathleen nodded, her mind racing. The evidence stacked before them, tangible proof of the animosity lurking beneath the veneer of friendly competition. They shared a glance, understanding the gravity of what lay in their hands. This was no longer just a mystery; it was a puzzle with pieces that could cut.

Carmella's fingers brushed a stray lock of hair from her face as she spread the letters across the coffee table. Kathleen and Frankie gathered close, their eyes roving over the venomous scrawl that spelled out threats against Tony. The air hung heavy with the scent of dust and tension.

"Deeper than we thought," Carmella murmured, her voice barely above a whisper. Her gaze locked onto a letter, its words slashing through any facade of civility among rivals.

"Look at these." Kathleen's hand shook as she laid the photographs next to the letters. Glossy images of pizzerias — some splashed with paint, others with windows smashed. A visual chronicle of hatred.

"Every picture... a story of anger," Frankie said, his broad hands flipping through the images. He stopped at one, Tony's face mid-shout, the veins in his neck bulging. "This wasn't just competition. It was war."

Carmella nodded, swallowing her anxiety, her mind whirring. "We've got to talk to them. The owners."

"Face-to-face?" Kathleen asked, her eyebrow arching, a flicker of mischief in her green eyes despite the gravity of the situation.

"Si," Frankie affirmed, his dark curls bouncing as he nodded. "Only way to see beyond the lies."

"Confrontation could be dangerous," Carmella warned, but her resolve was firm, her petite frame straightening with purpose.

"More dangerous than letting a killer walk free?" Kathleen countered, her lips pressed into a thin line.

"Then it's settled." Frankie's smile was gone, replaced by a steely determination. "We go to them. We find the truth."

They stood together, united in their quest, the cozy living room transformed into a staging ground for the battle ahead. Each knew what lay at stake. Each felt the weight of Tony's memory urging them on. They would unravel the tangled web of rivalries. They would seek justice.

Carmella's fingers trembled slightly as she raised her phone, the camera lens focusing on the slew of letters and photographs spread across the coffee table. Snap by snap, she captured the venomous words and violent imagery, each click echoing in the silent room like a promise to Tony to unveil his killer. She reviewed each photo for clarity, ensuring no detail was left to chance, then slid the device into her pocket with a soft thud against the fabric.

"Got everything?" Kathleen's voice cut through the concentrated silence.

"Every single shred," Carmella replied, her tone steady despite the quickened pulse at her neck.

Frankie glanced around the dimly lit living room, its walls once friendly and warm now seemed to close in with secrets. "This evidence... it's dynamite."

Kathleen stepped closer, her shadow melding with Carmella's. "We'll use it carefully. Can't afford any missteps now."

"Agreed," Carmella said, her gaze hardening. "Tony deserves that much."

The three of them moved in unison toward the front door, each step heavy with the weight of newfound responsibility. The air outside was crisp, the fading sun casting long shadows across the lawn as if nature itself held its breath for what would come next.

"Okay, team." Frankie's eyes met theirs, a silent pact passing between them. "Let's do this right. For Tony."

"Justice for Tony," Kathleen echoed, her face etched with resolute lines usually softened by laughter.

"Justice for Tony," Carmella affirmed, locking the door behind them with a decisive click.

They descended the porch steps, their silhouettes huddled together against the encroaching evening chill. With quiet determination, they made their way down the cobblestone path, their minds alive with strategy and speculation. They were a trio bound by purpose, inching ever closer to the heart of the mystery that gripped Wavecrest Cove. The truth was out there, shrouded in the shadows of rivalry and resentment. And they were determined to bring it to light.

Chapter 8

The kitchen hummed with silence, heavy with the day's work. Stainless steel surfaces gleamed under the fluorescent lights, and the stone oven exhaled a final breath of warmth. Detective Jones stood by the counter, his figure casting a long shadow across the black-and-white checkered tiles. Carmella eyed the curve of his back, the way his jacket stretched over broad shoulders.

"Quite a day," she murmured, her voice threading through the quiet like a cautious hand.

"Indeed," he replied without turning, his attention fixed on the notes scattered before him.

She inched closer, the scent of yeast and oregano mingling in the air between them. Her pulse thrummed a nervous rhythm against her wrist. The pizzeria, her inheritance and newfound purpose, had become an unexpected crime scene, yet in this moment, it felt more intimate than it ever had.

"Detective Jones..." Her words trailed off as she halted a mere step away from him, close enough to see the stubble lining his jaw, the weariness etched around his eyes.

Carmella watched his head tilt slightly, an indication he was listening despite the barriers he so carefully erected. She took a quiet breath, steadying herself for what needed to be said next, her resolve anchoring her to the spot.

Maddox felt the heat of her approach before he saw it, an unspoken question lingering in the air. He turned, an involuntary reaction to her proximity. Their eyes met—his blue gaze clashed with her deep brown stare, and something unspoken passed between them. He caught a glimpse of something more than just the determined investigator she presented to the world. His heart skipped, an unexpected guest in the rhythm of his pulse.

"Detective?" Carmella's voice held a note of hesitation, her usual confidence undercut by the uncertainty of this moment.

"Carmella," he acknowledged, his tone betraying none of the undercurrents swirling within. The skepticism that was his constant companion took a back seat, as if granting him a brief respite to simply be in the presence of another.

She reached forward. Her fingers grazed his arm, light as a whisper. It was a touch meant to comfort, perhaps to connect, yet it sparked a current that ran deeper than either intended. The contact was fleeting, but it lingered in the air, charged with a tension both subtle and undeniable.

"Sorry, I..." Carmella's voice trailed off, her gesture retreating as quickly as it had appeared, leaving behind a silence that spoke volumes.

Maddox's muscles tensed, his body recoiling almost imperceptibly. The contact of her skin against his was a jolt to his system, an electric reminder of the world outside their investigation. He stepped back, the ever-present cloak of skepticism resettling on his shoulders as he focused on the reality of their situation—a murder most foul and a killer still at large.

"Carmella, we can't," he said, his voice low, a blend of warning and regret. The scent of tomato sauce and basil lingered in the kitchen, a stark contrast to the seriousness of his tone.

Her hand fell away, a leaf caught in a sudden gust. She stepped back too, her eyes clouding with the realization of the line she'd nearly crossed. The warmth in them dimmed, replaced by the steel of professionalism.

"Right," she said, her voice steady once more. "The case." Her words were a life raft she clung to, pulling herself back from the emotional brink.

"Exactly," Maddox replied, his gaze locking onto hers, reinforcing the silent vow to keep their focus where it belonged—on justice.

Maddox shuffled backward, the worn tiles of the kitchen floor cool beneath his shoes. His jaw set firm, eyes narrowing as he reeled in his thoughts, corralling them back to the case at hand.

"Listen," he began, the word a businesslike barrier he erected between them. "We need to focus."

Carmella nodded, her mind a whirlwind of embarrassment and resolve. She squared her shoulders, pushing down the flutter in her chest.

"You're right. The investigation." Her voice was a beacon, cutting through the fog of unspoken words.

"Earlier today," she continued, her tone now all business, "I overheard one of the regulars talking about something odd they saw the night of..." She hesitated, then pushed on, "...the murder."

"Go on." Maddox's stance relaxed, imperceptibly, the detective in him surfacing at the promise of new information.

"Outside. Near the dumpster. It was late, but they mentioned a car they didn't recognize. Something about it felt off to them." Carmella's fingers drummed against the stainless steel countertop, betraying her eagerness.

"Did they see who was inside?" His voice held an edge of curiosity, skepticism momentarily shelved.

"No, but we could check if any nearby businesses have security cameras facing that lot." Carmella's suggestion hung in the air, a tangible thread in the complex web of their case.

"Good thinking," Maddox admitted, the investigator in him acknowledging her insight. "We'll follow up first thing."

"Agreed." Carmella's lips curved into a small, determined smile. They stood there, two silhouettes bathed in the fluorescent glow of the kitchen lights, their shared quest for truth bridging the gap that professionalism demanded.

Maddox's gaze lingered on Carmella, the detective in him watching as she paced the length of the kitchen, her petite frame a contrast to the towering pizza ovens that had cooled with the night. Her energy seemed to infuse the air, and despite his reservations, he found himself respecting her grit. She was not just the pizzeria owner; she was a force in her own right.

"Detective, there's something else," Carmella said, halting her steps. Her eyes locked onto his, a spark of insight flickering within their depths. "The regular, the one who saw the car—they also mentioned a key chain. A unique one. Dangling from the rear view mirror. It could be distinctive enough to identify the owner."

"Interesting." Maddox's stance softened, the lines of suspicion smoothing as he considered the potential lead. He watched her closely, noting the resolve etched into the fine lines of her face.

"Could it be significant?" she asked, her brows knitting together in concentration.

"Potentially," he conceded, the words measured yet sincere. The scent of basil and tomato sauce clung to the air, grounding him back in the present with the woman who stood before him as more than an incidental player in the investigation.

"Then we need to find out who that keychain belongs to," Carmella declared, the conviction in her voice clear and unyielding. Her suggestion carried the weight of a well-considered strategy.

"Agreed," Maddox replied, the corners of his mouth turning up ever so slightly in approval. Her tenacity was infectious; her dedication, admirable. Together, they began to weave through the labyrinth of clues, each step forward a shared endeavor toward uncovering the truth hidden within Wavecrest Cove.

Maddox nodded, the gears in his mind visibly turning. "Let's follow this up," he said, a newfound energy infusing his words. "We'll start first thing tomorrow."

"Thank you," Carmella breathed out, relief and anticipation mingling in her voice. She brushed a stray lock of hair from her forehead, her movements betraying a subtle eagerness.

Side by side, they surveyed the quiet kitchen, the stainless steel surfaces gleaming under the fluorescent lights. The day's frenzy had settled into a hush, leaving only the hum of the refrigerator to fill the silence.

"Strange, isn't it?" Carmella mused, her gaze drifting across the room. "How life goes on around... even when so much is at stake."

"Indeed." Maddox's reply was soft, almost reflective. In the dimming light, his sharp features seemed less imposing, more human.

They stepped through the threshold, leaving the scent of oregano and garlic behind. The chill of the evening air greeted them, an abrupt contrast to the warmth of the kitchen. They walked, their footsteps synchronized against the pavement.

"Today was..." Carmella's voice trailed off, searching for the right words.

"Productive," Maddox finished for her, glancing sideways. Their eyes met, held. A shared understanding passed between them, fleeting yet profound.

"Productive," she echoed, a small smile playing on her lips.

The moment lingered, then dissolved as they refocused on the path ahead, the unspoken bond between them tucked away like a secret, ready to be revisited when the time was right.

They rounded the corner, a brisk pace marking their progress through the shadow-strewn streets of Wavecrest Cove. Maddox's gaze lingered on Carmella for an instant, noting how she navigated the cobblestones with a sure-footed grace that belied her recent city life.

"Back there, in Nonna's kitchen," he began, his voice steady, "you pieced together fragments I'd overlooked."

"Instinct," she replied, brushing off the compliment. "Or maybe it's just Nonna's spirit guiding me."

A chuckle escaped him, rare and genuine. He watched the lamplight dance in her eyes, igniting flecks of gold. Maddox had built walls, brick by professional brick, but admiration seeped through the cracks. Carmella'squick wit was not just intuition; it was intelligence honed by years in a cutthroat world he knew little about.

"Instinct has its place," he conceded, "but that was skill."

She met his gaze, and in the depths of those blue eyes, she found an ally. Her shoulders squared, resolve crystallizing within her. She felt capable, emboldened by the acknowledgment from a man who made a career of doubting.

"Let's go over the witness list again," she suggested, her words crisp in the evening air. "Someone saw something, I'm sure of it."

"Lead the way," Maddox said, motioning forward.

Their strides matched as they delved deeper into the heart of the investigation, shoulder to shoulder. In the cool night, their breaths mingled, visible puffs of shared determination. Carmella'stheory unfolded, each detail sharp and clear. Maddox listened, the detective in him dissecting her every word, finding no fault.

"Good work, Carmella," he affirmed, and the weight of his approval fortified her spirit.

Together, they were more than solitary figures chasing shadows; they were a team, their collective insight piercing the veil of mystery that shrouded Wavecrest Cove.

Carmella rifled through the stack of papers, her brow furrowed in concentration. The fluorescent lights hummed above them, casting a stark glow over the stainless steel counters and checkerboard floor of 'Nonna's

Slice of Heaven.' Detective Jones leaned against the wall, his arms folded, his gaze fixed on the documents sprawled across the tabletop.

"Anything?" he asked, breaking the silence that had settled between them like an unspoken agreement.

"Maybe," Carmella replied, tapping a fingertip on a crinkled receipt. "This delivery order—it was placed just minutes before the murder."

Maddox straightened, the subtle crease in his forehead deepening. His eyes, sharp as ever, scanned the receipt. "Time-stamped and paid in cash. Could be something."

Their hands brushed as they both reached for the paper, a jolt of electricity passing through the brief contact. They withdrew in unison, a silent acknowledgment of the line they could not cross. Not here. Not now.

"Right," Carmella said, her voice steady, though her heart betrayed her with its erratic beat. "Focus, we need to focus."

"Agreed," Maddox responded, the corner of his mouth twitching as if fighting back a smile that had no place in the gravity of their task.

They poured over the details, piecing together timelines and motives with methodical precision. The kitchen's lingering scent of oregano and tomato sauce became a backdrop to their shared pursuit. Words flowed between them, concise, each one building upon the last, a bridge made of theories and facts.

"Could this delivery guy be our witness?" Maddox mused aloud, his blue eyes glinting with the reflection of a new angle.

"Or our suspect." Carmella's voice held an edge of possibility. She leaned in closer, her mind racing.

He nodded, the detective in him alive with the thrill of the chase. "We'll find out tomorrow. We'll question him."

"First thing," Carmella agreed, pushing aside the flutter in her chest, the awareness of his proximity.

"First thing," he echoed, standing shoulder to shoulder with her, their gazes locked on the path ahead. There was a crime to solve, a truth to uncover, and nothing else could stand in their way—not even the unspoken words that hung in the air, charged and waiting.

Chapter 9

Carmella barged into Kathleen's cozy, cluttered living room unannounced. The scent of old books and jasmine tea hung in the air. She found Kathleen nestled in an overstuffed armchair, a mystery novel splayed open in her lap.

"Kathleen," Carmella said, her voice sharp as she clutched the back of a nearby sofa for support. "We need to talk. Now."

Kathleen glanced up, her green eyes widening in surprise. A bookmark slid between the pages as she closed the book with a gentle thud. "Carmella? What's wrong?"

"It's about Tony." Carmella's fingers dug into the floral fabric of the sofa, her knuckles whitening. "You dated him, didn't you? And you never told me."

Kathleen's face softened, a tinge of guilt flashing across her features before she composed herself. She stood, crossing the room to stand before Carmella. "Yes, I did date Tony," she confessed, meeting Carmella's gaze steadily. "But it was a long time ago, way before he became your competition."

"Before he was murdered," Carmella added, the last word catching in her throat.

"Before that too," Kathleen quickly reassured her. "Look, what happened between Tony and me has no bearing on what's going on now. It ended cleanly, and we moved on."

"Cleanly?" Carmella echoed, her heart pounding against her ribs. "Then why keep it a secret?"

"Because it was irrelevant," Kathleen insisted, her voice firm yet tinged with empathy. "I didn't want to dredge up the past or cause any unnecessary drama."

Carmella's chest heaved as she tried to process the information, the betrayal stinging like a fresh wound. She watched Kathleen's face for any sign of deceit, but all she saw was the earnest concern of a friend who had been caught withholding the truth.

Carmella paced the length of the room, her footsteps muffled by the woven rug. The air felt thick with tension, and she could taste the faint bitterness of betrayal on her tongue. A stray sunbeam caught the dust dancing in the silence between them.

"Kathleen, how do I know this is all?" Carmella asked, her voice a mixture of hurt and suspicion.

Kathleen's hands clutched together, her knuckles pale. "Because I'm telling you, Carmella. We're friends—best friends. Secrets about old flames don't change that."

"Best friends don't keep secrets," Carmella countered, her eyes searching Kathleen's. The aroma of aged paper and ink from the nearby bookshelf seemed to underscore the gravity of their conversation.

"Carmella, please." Kathleen stepped closer, her shadow falling over the coffee table. "I never meant to hurt you. This was just... It was years ago. It has nothing to do with Tony's death or us."

Carmella halted, her back turned to shield her wavering resolve. She heard the earnest plea in Kathleen's voice, sensed the truth mingling with regret.

"Believe in what we have," Kathleen continued, her tone softening. "I would never betray your trust. Not now, not ever."

Carmella's breath hitched. She wanted to believe, to erase the gnawing doubt that had rooted itself in her chest. Her shoulders slumped as she fought against the urge to yield to Kathleen's assurance. It wasn't easy, piecing together the fragments of trust once they had been scattered.

"Okay," Carmella whispered, allowing the word to hang in the air, a tentative step towards mending the rift that had formed between them.

Carmella edged away from the table, her hands trembling slightly as she wrapped her cardigan tighter around herself. She glanced at Kathleen, whose gaze lingered with a mix of hope and fear. "I need to think," Carmella muttered, almost to herself.

"Of course, take all the time you need," Kathleen replied, but her words were lost to Carmella's retreat.

The door closed behind her with a soft click, sealing off the library's sanctuary of secrets. Outside, the crisp autumn air nipped at Carmella's cheeks, painting them a light pink. She walked, each step deliberate, away from the comforting walls of knowledge and into the embrace of Wavecrest Cove's quaint streets.

Alone now, Carmella allowed the floodgates to open. Memories surged. Laughter shared over steaming cups of cocoa. Confidences exchanged under starlit skies. Had there been shadows lurking beneath Kathleen's bright smile?

She found herself outside Nonna's Slice of Heaven. The pizzeria stood silent, an anchor in her tempest-tossed world. Carmella peered through the glass, at the familiar checkered tablecloths and gleaming counters. It was here, amidst flour and tomato sauce, that Kathleen had cheered her on, each success celebrated, each failure consoled.

"Was it all genuine?" she whispered, her breath fogging up the windowpane.

A gust of wind brushed past, carrying with it the scent of oregano and thyme. Carmella shivered, wrapping her arms around herself. Could she have missed the signs? Those moments when Kathleen's eyes darted away, or when her laughter came too quick and sharp?

"Focus on what you know," Carmella chided herself, drawing strength from the town's steady heartbeat. This was not about betrayal. This was about finding the truth.

"Truth," Carmella repeated, her conviction growing stronger. She would not let doubt cloud her judgment. Not without proof. Not without reason.

With a deep breath, Carmella pushed away from the window. She turned towards home, steps resolute. There would be time for reflection, for sifting through memories. But first, she needed space to breathe, to think, to heal. Only then could she face Kathleen, their friendship, and the gnarled roots of Tony's untimely demise.

Carmella paced the length of her living room, her steps muffled by the thick rug underfoot. The grandfather clock in the corner ticked away, a steady reminder of time slipping through her fingers. She stopped by the mantel, running a finger over the framed photo of herself and Kathleen at last year's Fourth of July picnic. They had been inseparable then, as they had for so many years.

"Strange," she muttered, recalling the day Kathleen had canceled their weekly book club at the last minute. No reason given, just a vague apology. It was unlike Kathleen to be so evasive. And that time at the library, when Carmella had found her whispering on the phone, her usual open-book demeanor replaced with hushed urgency. Kathleen had laughed it off, but the laughter hadn't reached her green eyes.

Carmella sank into her armchair, pulling a knit blanket around her shoulders. She considered the evidence that had surfaced – the torn page from Tony's diary found tucked in a library book, the anonymous tip that led to the discovery of Tony's heirloom watch in Kathleen's garden. Coincidences? Or something more?

"Years of friendship," she whispered to the quiet room. Their past was woven with shared confidences and support. Kathleen had been there when Carmella's grandfather passed, holding her hand through the grief. She had championed Carmella's every idea for the pizzeria, even the ones that flopped.

"Could she really be involved?" Doubt gnawed at her resolve. The image of Kathleen's face, so full of sincerity, warred with the mounting suspicions. Carmella's heart ached with the conflict.

"Proof," she said aloud. A weighty word, demanding attention. Carmella needed answers, solid and irrefutable. Until then, she would hold onto the memories of their deep-rooted bond, hoping they were enough to keep the shadow of distrust at bay.

Carmella rose from the armchair, the knit blanket slipping from her shoulders. Her feet carried her to the window, where she pressed a palm against the cool glass, gazing out over Wavecrest Cove. The town was settling into the evening lull, lights twinkling like distant stars fallen to earth.

"Without proof," she murmured, "it's just shadows and doubt."

A deep breath filled her lungs, carrying the salty tang of the sea. It steadied her. She couldn't – wouldn't – let suspicion tear the seams of a friendship stitched through years of loyalty and laughter. Not without something more substantial than whispers and circumstantial finds.

The pizzeria called to her, a beacon in the growing dusk. Nonna's Slice of Heaven, with its checkered tablecloths and oven's warm embrace, promised refuge. Carmella grabbed her keys, locked the door behind her, and made her way down the cobblestone path.

She pushed open the door to the aroma of tomatoes and dough. The familiar sound of sizzling cheese greeted her ears. At the counter, Mario, her assistant, flashed a grin.

"Hey, boss lady! You're late for the dinner rush."

Mama Mia It's Murder

"Sorry, Mario," Carmella replied, tying on her apron with practiced ease. "Just needed some air."

"Anything I can do?" Concern laced his words. He knew her well enough to read her moods.

"Keep those pizzas flying," she said, squeezing his shoulder as she passed by.

The rhythm of work enveloped her. Rolling dough. Spreading sauce. A sprinkle of basil here, a handful of mozzarella there. The oven's heat flushed her cheeks. Laughter bubbled from the dining area, where families gathered around tables, sharing slices and stories.

"Carmella!" Old Mrs. Henderson called from her usual booth, waving a hand. "You've outdone yourself with this pie!"

"Thank you, Mrs. Henderson," Carmella smiled, genuinely warmed by the compliment.

As she moved among the patrons, refilling drinks and exchanging pleasantries, the threads of community wove around her, strengthening the fabric of her resolve. These were her people, her anchor. They trusted her, relied on her. She couldn't let them down.

"Any news on the case?" Mr. Jenkins asked, lowering his voice. His eyes held a mix of curiosity and concern.

"Still working on it," Carmella replied, careful to keep her tone neutral. "But thank you for asking, Mr. Jenkins."

Back at the counter, she paused, watching the townspeople. Their support, unspoken but palpable, buoyed her spirits. Kathleen had been a part of that tapestry too, her thread interlaced with Carmella's in a pattern of shared history.

"Can't let this tear us apart," Carmella whispered to herself. "Not yet."

With each pizza served, each smile exchanged, her conviction solidified. She would find the truth, but she would not sacrifice a friendship on the altar of hearsay. Not without proof. Not without knowing, beyond a shadow of a doubt, that Kathleen had crossed the line from friend to foe.

The bell above Nonna's Slice of Heaven's entrance tinkled. Carmella glanced up, her hands dusted with flour. Kathleen stood at the threshold, her silhouette framed by the setting sun. The glow cast fiery highlights in her red hair, giving her an almost ethereal appearance. But her eyes, usually dancing with mischief, now held a somber weight.

"Carmella," Kathleen began, her voice low, "I owe you an apology."

Carmella wiped her hands on her apron and stepped closer, her movements hesitant. She met Kathleen's gaze, searching for the friend she knew.

"Tony and I... It was a long time ago. I should've told you," Kathleen continued, her words tumbling out.

"Kathleen," Carmella interrupted, her brow furrowed, "why now? Why not before?"

Kathleen's shoulders slumped. "Fear, I guess. Fear of losing you. But secrets, they're like splinters, aren't they? Sooner or later, they work their way to the surface."

Carmella took in Kathleen's remorseful stance, the tension in her slender frame. A maelstrom of emotions churned within her; trust warring with doubt, the past clashing with the present.

"Your loyalty means everything to me, Kathleen. But this... It's hard."

"I know, and I'm so sorry." Kathleen's green eyes shimmered, a testament to her sincerity. "But I'm here for you, always have been."

"Always?" Carmella echoed, her heart aching with the need to believe.

"Always," Kathleen affirmed, her voice steady.

The pizzeria hummed with the sound of conversation and the aroma of baking pizza. Life moved around them, oblivious to the crossroads at which two friends stood.

"Okay," Carmella said finally, her voice barely above a whisper, her decision made amidst the scent of oregano and melted cheese. "We'll get through this. Together."

Their eyes locked, an unspoken pact forming between them. Forgiveness wouldn't come easy; trust would need to be rebuilt, one truth at a time. But the first step had been taken, a step toward clearing the haze of suspicion that had settled over Wavecrest Cove.

"Thank you, Carmella," Kathleen breathed, relief washing over her features.

"Don't thank me yet," Carmella replied with a half-smile. "We've got a murderer to catch, remember?"

Kathleen nodded, the hint of a smile tugging at her lips. "Right behind you, partner."

Together, they turned back toward the lively pizzeria, the warmth from the oven wrapping around them like a promise. The future was uncertain, the path ahead fraught with questions. But for now, they stood united, ready to face whatever lay hidden in the shadows of Wavecrest Cove.

Carmella wiped her hands on a dish towel and placed two steaming mugs of herbal tea on the checkered tablecloth. The pizzeria emptied, leaving an echo behind every footfall. She settled across from Kathleen, her gaze holding a mixture of warmth and wary curiosity.

"Talk to me, Kathleen," Carmella urged, her voice steady despite the storm of emotions within. "I need to know what you're feeling, too."

Kathleen wrapped her fingers around the mug, the heat seeping into her skin. Her green eyes met Carmella's, unshielded for once. "I'm scared," she admitted, her voice a thread of vulnerability. "Scared you'll look at me one day and see someone you can't trust."

"Trust is... It's not just given; it's built," Carmella said, tracing the rim of her own mug. "It's brick by brick, Kathleen. And when one gets removed, the whole thing feels shaky."

"Like Jenga," Kathleen offered with a weak chuckle, trying to lighten the moment.

"Exactly like Jenga," Carmella agreed, allowing a small smile. "But we're more than a game. We've got history. And I want to believe in that."

"History doesn't erase mistakes," Kathleen murmured, looking down.

"No, it doesn't. But it gives us something to work with," Carmella replied. She took a deep breath. "Forgiveness isn't instant, Kat. It's a journey. And if you're willing, I am too."

"Journeys are better with company," Kathleen said, a hopeful note lacing her words.

"Then let's take it one step at a time," Carmella proposed, reaching across the table. Her hand hovered, then settled over Kathleen's. "Together."

"Thank you, Carmella," Kathleen whispered, her grip firm and reassuring.

"Let's start with honesty. All cards on the table. Always," Carmella affirmed.

"Always," Kathleen echoed, nodding in agreement. They sat in silence, letting the weight of their words settle between them like the dust motes dancing in the shafts of light from the overhead lamp.

Carmella rose, her movements brisk and decisive. The chair scraped against the floorboards—a sharp contrast to the hushed tones that had filled the room moments before. She paced to the window, gaze settling on the quiet street of Wavecrest Cove where the pizzeria stood, a beacon of warmth in the dimming light.

"Tony's murder won't solve itself," Carmella said, more to herself than to Kathleen. The reflection in the glass showed her friend still seated, watching her with an intensity that matched the seriousness of their task.

"No," Kathleen agreed, rising to join Carmella at the window. "It won't."

They stood shoulder to shoulder, their reflection mingling with the view outside. Carmella turned, her eyes meeting Kathleen's directly. "We need to dig deeper, get our hands dirty if we have to."

Kathleen nodded, her red hair catching the last rays of the sunset. "And we'll do it together. Like we always have."

"Partners?" Carmella extended her hand, not just in gesture but as a symbol of their renewed alliance.

"Partners." Kathleen clasped Carmella's hand, sealing the pact. Their handshake was firm, a physical testament to their commitment.

"We follow the evidence," Carmella stated, releasing Kathleen's hand and moving toward the bookshelf that housed an assortment of detective novels alongside cookbooks. "No matter where it leads."

"Agreed." Kathleen's voice held a steel edge, belying her usual levity. Her green eyes shone with determination.

"Let's start first thing tomorrow," Carmella suggested, pulling out a notepad and pen from among the books. She scribbled a quick list, each point a step forward in their quest for truth.

"First light," Kathleen confirmed, peering over Carmella's shoulder at the burgeoning plan. "I'll bring coffee."

"Make it strong," Carmella replied, a small smile tugging at her lips despite the gravity of the situation.

"Always." Kathleen's tone carried a promise, one far deeper than caffeine.

The evening settled around them like a cloak, the world outside retreating as they drew up chairs and leaned over the notepad. Together in silence, they strategized, each point on paper a shared vow to uncover the truth behind Tony's untimely demise. Their friendship had weathered storms before; this time, it would navigate them through the mystery that lay ahead.

Chapter 10

The moon cast a pale glow over Tony's pizzeria as Carmella and Kathleen slipped through the back door. It creaked softly, betraying their entrance into the silent kitchen where stainless steel counters gleamed in the dim light.

"Quick and quiet," Carmella whispered, her eyes scanning the room for any signs of disturbance. Her fingers fidgeted with her sleeve, a nervous tick that surfaced whenever she delved into the unknown.

"Like ghosts," Kathleen replied, her voice barely above a breath as her green eyes danced with mischief. She moved with a fluid grace, her notepad ready in hand.

They worked in tandem, Carmella snapping photos with her phone while Kathleen scribbled notes. The aroma of garlic and tomato sauce lingered, a ghost of busy dinners past. They searched methodically, under tables, behind the soda fountain, every nook a potential clue holder.

Carmella's heart thumped louder as they approached Tony's office. The door swung inward, revealing a shrine to a life kneaded by dough and tradition. Certificates adorned the walls alongside faded photographs of Tony, his stocky frame ever-present even now.

"Desk," Kathleen murmured, pointing.

Carmella nodded, crossing the room to the mahogany behemoth that dominated the space. Drawers slid open smoothly, files and receipts piled neatly within. Routine. Expected. But Carmella's instincts itched for more.

She examined the desk closer, her fingers grazing over the wood grain until—click. A false bottom sprung free, revealing its secret bounty. Carmella's breath hitched as she drew out a stack of letters, each one more threatening than the last.

"Kathleen, look at this." Carmella's voice trembled, the weight of discovery heavy in her hands.

"Tony, oh Tony, what were you tangled in?" Kathleen leaned in, her eyes skimming the angry scrawl on the pages.

"Jason Keller... Otto Marks," Carmella read aloud, her pulse quickening as names tied to rumors now linked to tangible threats.

"Deep trouble," Kathleen murmured, her humor evaporating into solemnity.

Carmella's resolve hardened. Tony's rivalry with the other pizzeria owners had been more than petty squabbles over pizza crust thickness. There was malice here, seeping through inked words and unspoken vendettas.

"Let's get these documented," Carmella said, her determination fueling action. "We need to know exactly what we're dealing with."

"Agreed," Kathleen replied, the click of her pen a sharp note in the quiet office.

Evidence in tow, they left as they came—silent shadows among the lingering scent of oregano and dough.

The bell above the coffee shop door jangled as Carmella and Kathleen entered. They spotted Jason Keller immediately, his slicked-back hair gleaming under the warm light, a stark contrast to the cozy ambiance of the café. He sat alone at a corner table, a neat espresso before him, untouched.

"Jason," Carmella began, wasting no time on pleasantries, "we need to talk."

His thin mustache twitched with a hint of annoyance. "Ladies," he greeted, voice dripping sarcasm. "To what do I owe this unexpected pleasure?"

"Tony's letters," Kathleen cut in, her tone brisk. She slid into the seat opposite him, her eyes locked on his. "They paint a picture, Jason. A troubling one."

Jason leaned back, his flashy jacket crinkling. "Letters?" he feigned confusion, a calculated move. "You'll have to be more specific."

Carmella produced the photographs from her purse, spreading them out like cards on the table. The evidence was clear. His name, Otto's, threats all too explicit. "These," she said firmly. "Addressed to Tony. Ring any bells?"

"Ah," Jason sighed theatrically, examining the images. "Rivalry makes people say silly things." He waved a dismissive hand, his facade of indifference unshaken.

"Was it just 'silly things', or did it go further?" Kathleen pressed, her gaze sharp as a blade.

"Purely professional," Jason declared, finally meeting their stares. "Competition is the lifeblood of business, after all."

"Is that why Tony's dead?" Carmella probed, her voice steady.

"Accusing me?" His laughter was short, scornful. "I have no part in such... messiness."

Carmella watched him closely. There it was—a flicker in his eyes, a brief dance of shadows across his face. Fear? Guilt? It was gone as quick as it had appeared, but it was enough. Enough for doubt to take root.

"Of course," Carmella said, her decision made. "Thank you for your time, Jason."

They rose, leaving him with his untouched espresso and a glint of unease. Outside, the chill air bit at their cheeks, but inside, the fire of suspicion burned hotter than ever.

Carmella flipped through the dusty archives, each page a whisper of history in the dimly lit room. The scent of old paper mingled with the mustiness of the space, a repository of Wavecrest Cove's collective memory. Kathleen, perched on a wooden stool beside her, rifled through stacks of records, her fingers swift and sure.

"Anything yet?" Carmella asked, squinting at the faded print on a yellowed newspaper clipping.

Kathleen shook her head, her long red hair catching the light. "Just routine articles. Festivals, bake sales... Ah, here's something about a dog that could skateboard."

Carmella chuckled despite the tension coiling in her stomach. "Keep looking. There has to be something we can use against Jason Keller." Her voice lowered instinctively, even though the archive room was empty save for them.

Minutes ticked by, marked only by the rustle of papers and the occasional creak of shelves settling under the weight of time. Then, Kathleen stilled, her green eyes widening. "Carmella, look at this."

She slid an article across the table, its headline bold even after years of obscurity: 'Local Restaurateur Sues Rival for Sabotage.' Carmella leaned in, absorbing every word. The report detailed Jason Keller's unscrupulous tactics, how he'd been accused of tampering with another chef's ingredients, leading to a disastrous health inspection.

"Got you," Carmella muttered under her breath, her pulse quickening. She met Kathleen's gaze, seeing reflected there the same steely resolve.

"Think he'd do it again?" Kathleen's question hung between them, heavy with implications.

"Wouldn't put it past him," Carmella replied, her mind racing. Tony's pizzeria, their confrontation with Jason, the veiled threats—it all pointed to a man who played dirty to stay on top.

"Let's go talk to some of these former employees," Kathleen suggested, already rising from her seat. "They might have more dirt on our Mr. Keller."

Carmella nodded, folding the article with care and tucking it into her bag. Evidence. Motive. Now they needed testimony to piece together the sinister puzzle of rivalry and revenge that had claimed Tony's life.

They left the archives, the door closing with a soft click behind them. The evening air greeted them with a crisp chill, but the trail they were on promised to grow only hotter.

Carmella slipped into the bustling event, her gaze sweeping over the crowd. She blended in, another curious onlooker amidst the throng of Jason Keller's admirers. The scent of rich spices and sizzling gourmet creations filled the air, a testament to the culinary spectacle before them. She edged closer to the front, where Jason held court.

"Ah, our local gastronomic wizard," she murmured, close enough now to catch his eye.

"Welcome!" Jason's voice cut through the din, sharp as a chef's knife. "You seem new to my little soirées. What brings you here?"

"Curiosity," Carmella said, offering a smile that didn't quite reach her eyes. "Heard you're the man to know for good food around here."

"Only the best," he boasted, his mustache twitching with pride. "So, what can I do for you?"

"Actually," Carmella ventured, her voice casual, "I was wondering about your competition. Like Tony's pizzeria?"

"Ah, Tony," Jason's lips curled into a tight smirk. "Tragic what happened. But business is business, and mine is thriving."

"Was it just business between you two?" Carmella prodded, watching his reaction.

"Purely professional rivalry." Jason's response came quick, too quick.

"Of course," Carmella nodded, pretending to be convinced.

In the corner of her eye, she caught Otto Marks' entrance. He navigated the space with quiet authority, his gaze landing on Jason. They shared a fleeting look, an exchange so brief most would miss it. But not Carmella. It was a silent conversation, and her heart skipped a beat.

"Enjoy the evening," Jason said, moving on to charm another guest.

"Thank you, I will," Carmella replied, her focus shifting. She watched as Otto made his way to a secluded spot, Jason joining him moments later. Their heads leaned in, words exchanged in hushed tones. Carmella's mind raced. The article, the lawsuit, now this covert meeting—it all painted a sinister picture.

She backed away, blending once more into the crowd. The pieces were coming together, but the puzzle wasn't quite complete. She needed more, and she would get it. For Tony. For justice. Carmella was certain now; the truth lay hidden within the secret rivalry that simmered beneath the surface of Wavecrest Cove's culinary scene.

The evening air nipped at Carmella's cheeks as she and Kathleen slipped out of the event, their eyes trained on Otto Marks' departing figure. They maintained a safe distance, blending with the shadows that clung to the quaint streets of Wavecrest Cove. Otto moved with purpose, his gait steady, unaware of the two women mirroring his path.

"Keep your camera ready," Carmella whispered, her voice barely louder than the rustling leaves overhead. Kathleen nodded, her fingers poised over the device in her pocket.

They rounded a corner to see Otto unlocking the back entrance of his pizzeria, "Marks of Excellence." Light spilled out onto the darkened alley as he stepped inside, the door closing with a soft click behind him. Carmella and Kathleen crept closer, peering through a gap in the curtains. Otto was alone, moving about with an efficiency that spoke of long hours spent in the kitchen.

"Let's go in," Kathleen suggested, her voice low but laced with excitement. "Time for some undercover pizza tasting."

Carmella agreed, and they circled around to the front, entering under the guise of late-night customers. The warm scent of baking dough and tomato sauce enveloped them. Otto looked up from kneading dough, his expression unreadable behind those thin glasses.

"Evening, ladies. What can I get for you?" His tone was polite, but his eyes held a hint of suspicion.

"Two slices of your best pizza, please," Carmella said, her smile friendly as she leaned on the counter. "We've heard great things."

"Only the best here," Otto replied, sliding a pie into the oven with practiced ease.

Kathleen busied herself with examining the framed photos on the walls while Carmella engaged Otto. "You must have been shocked by Tony's passing. Terrible business, that."

"Shocked, yes," Otto responded, his face a mask of professionalism. "But life goes on, doesn't it?"

"Indeed, it does. Did you and Tony have any... disagreements that we should know about? We're new to town, just trying to understand the local history."

"Disagreements?" Otto's eyebrow lifted ever so slightly. "Nothing more than the usual competition. It keeps us all sharp, wouldn't you say?"

"Of course," Carmella nodded, watching as he sliced the steaming pizza and plated it with deft movements. She could sense the careful control in his words, the way he navigated the conversation like one might handle delicate pastry.

"Here you are," Otto said, presenting them with the slices. "Enjoy."

"Thank you," Kathleen chimed in, her tone light. "It looks delicious."

They settled at a table near the window, their backs to the wall, allowing them to observe Otto's every move. As they ate, they exchanged glances, their shared suspicion unspoken yet palpable.

"Delicious indeed," Carmella commented, loud enough for Otto to hear. "You're quite the craftsman with your pizza."

"Years of practice," Otto replied, a trace of pride in his voice.

"Must be tough, carrying on after losing a fellow chef like Tony," Carmella prodded gently, watching for any flicker of emotion.

"Tony had his place, and I have mine," Otto stated flatly. "That's how this town works. Everyone finds their niche."

"Sounds like a healthy rivalry to me," Carmella mused, her gaze never leaving Otto's face.

"Exactly." Otto's reply came quick, his eyes locking with hers for a fleeting moment before he turned away to tend to the oven.

Carmella and Kathleen shared a look, their plates now empty. Their mission for the night was complete, but the puzzle of Tony's untimely demise remained unsolved. They rose to leave, offering thanks and compliments to their host, who watched them go with an unreadable expression.

"Goodnight, Mr. Marks," Carmella called out as they departed. "Maybe we'll see you again soon."

"Goodnight," Otto replied, his voice echoing faintly in the now quiet pizzeria.

Carmella leaned forward, her voice soft but insistent. "Otto, such a tragedy about Tony," she said, threading concern into her words.

"Tragic indeed," Otto responded, his hands clasped neatly on the table.

"Must shake up the whole dynamic around here, right?" Kathleen chimed in, her eyes scanning for any skip in Otto's composed rhythm.

"Business is business," Otto shrugged, a well-rehearsed line delivered with a cool detachment. But then, just as he sipped his water, Carmella caught it—the tiniest hitch in his stoic facade, a micro-tremor that danced across his brow. It was gone as quickly as it appeared, but it was there—a crack in the veneer.

"Of course," Carmella murmured, exchanging a glance with Kathleen.

They stood, their chairs scraping softly against the floor. "Thank you for the pizza, Otto. It really is exceptional," Carmella offered with a smile, her mind already racing with questions.

"Thank you for coming," Otto replied, his gaze following them to the door.

Outside, under the dim glow of streetlamps, Carmella and Kathleen walked in step, their breaths visible in the crisp night air. They turned down the sidewalk, away from the warm light spilling out of Otto's pizzeria.

"Did you see it?" Carmella asked, her voice low.

"His reaction? Absolutely," Kathleen confirmed. "It was like a shadow passed over him for just a second."

"Too brief for him to fake." Carmella's mind buzzed with the implications. "We're onto something."

"Agreed. But we need more—hard evidence."

"Tomorrow," Carmella decided, the determination in her eyes reflecting the resolve in her voice. "We start digging deeper."

"Let's do it," Kathleen said, her stride purposeful as they vanished into the night, leaving the quiet piazza behind, their thoughts fixed on the unfolding mystery of Tony's murder.

The bell above the door chimed softly as Carmella and Kathleen stepped into the familiar warmth of "Nonna's Slice of Heaven". They moved with quiet efficiency, slipping off their coats and setting them on a nearby chair. The pizzeria, devoid of its usual bustle, felt like a sanctuary to them now—a base for their clandestine operation.

"Let's lay everything out," Carmella said, her voice hushed but firm. She unzipped her bag and began placing photographs and notes across the checkered tablecloth. Kathleen joined in, arranging the evidence with a practiced hand, each item a piece of the puzzle they were determined to solve.

"Threatening letters, that flinch from Otto, and now this old lawsuit against Keller..." Kathleen mused, tapping a finger against her lips. "It's like a spider web, and we're finding the sticky threads."

Carmella nodded, her eyes scanning the array of documents. "Connections are forming." Her fingertip traced lines between names and dates, her brow furrowed in concentration. "We need to anticipate their next move."

"Which means getting ahead of the game," Kathleen added, pulling up a chair and sitting down opposite Carmella. "Tomorrow, we hit the ground running."

"Exactly. We confront the truth, no matter where it leads." Carmella's resolve was palpable, her petite frame exuding a strength that filled the empty pizzeria.

The clock ticked away the minutes as they reviewed their findings into the night, whispering theories and counterpoints. They worked tirelessly, fueled by the need for answers, until the moon hung high in the sky.

As the night waned, Carmella's phone buzzed against the wooden tabletop, breaking the silence. She glanced at the screen. An unknown number. Curiosity piqued, she answered.

"Hello?" Her voice carried a cautious curiosity.

"Carmella Moretti?" The voice on the other end was distorted, a deliberate attempt to mask identity.

"Yes. Who is this?"

"Someone who knows what happened to Tony. Meet me tomorrow. Noon. Wavecrest Park." The line went dead before Carmella could respond.

She set the phone down slowly, her gaze meeting Kathleen's. "That was someone claiming to have information on Tony's murder."

"Anonymous tip?" Kathleen raised an eyebrow, her green eyes sharp with intrigue.

"Seems like it. Wants to meet at Wavecrest Park at noon." She tapped her phone thoughtfully.

"Could be our break—or a trap," Kathleen stated, her tone even but her posture alert.

"Either way, we can't ignore it." Carmella stood up, determination etched into her features. "Tomorrow, we might just find the missing piece we've been looking for."

"Then let's get some rest. We'll need to be sharp." Kathleen rose, her expression mirroring Carmella's resolve.

They gathered their things, leaving the table strewn with breadcrumbs of evidence and the promise of a new lead. As they turned off the lights and locked the door behind them, the darkness of the night seemed a little less impenetrable, their shared purpose a beacon guiding them forward.

Chapter 11

The corridor was silent, the sound of their steps a stark cadence in the stillness. Carmella and Detective Jones approached the lacquered door of Jason Keller's residence, their movements precise, their intentions clear.

A rap on the door, firm but not aggressive. Seconds crawled by. A lock clicked, hinges groaned, and the door swung open to reveal the man in question. Jason Keller stood framed in the doorway, his slicked-back hair gleaming under the hallway light, the thin mustache above his lip twitching slightly as if to accentuate his smirk.

"Detective Jones, Miss Moretti," he greeted, voice dripping with condescension.

Carmella scanned him from head to toe, taking in the ostentatious silk shirt that clung to his torso, the trousers that were just a touch too tight, the shine on his shoes rivaling that of his hair. His whole being radiated smugness.

"Jason," Detective Jones's greeting was curt, the single word heavy with unspoken scrutiny.

"May we come in?" Carmella asked, her tone steady, betraying none of the repulsion she felt at the sight before her.

"By all means," Jason gestured grandly, stepping aside.

As they passed him, Carmella could almost feel the cloud of arrogance that enveloped Jason, as tangible as the cologne that filled her nostrils. She moved forward, determined to cut through the façade, to find the truth that lay beneath.

They stepped across the threshold into Jason's living room. The scent of rich mahogany mixed with a hint of lemon polish assaulted their senses. Eyes darted around, taking in the gold-leaf frames that adorned the walls, each boasting an article that sang Jason's praises in bold print.

"Quite the shrine," Detective Jones muttered, his voice dry as parchment.

Carmella perched on the edge of a velvet armchair that seemed too pristine for comfort. Its royal blue hue clashed with the scarlet drapes behind it—every item in the room screamed for attention. Detective Jones, meanwhile, found a sturdy bookshelf to lean on. He crossed his arms, the fabric of his jacket stretching taut over his muscles, a silent sentinel amidst the sea of culinary accolades.

The air hung heavy, charged with the weight of unsaid words and unasked questions.

Carmella leaned forward, elbows resting lightly on her knees. "Let's talk about Tony Bianco," she started, eyes fixed on Jason as she brushed a stray lock of hair behind her ear.

Jason chuckled, his back straightening against the door he had just closed. "Tony?" His voice oozed disbelief. "What about him?"

"Your relationship with him," Carmella continued, unphased. "We're aware there were... let's call them tensions."

The smirk that curled Jason's thin mustache seemed to mock the very air it sliced through. He took slow steps toward an ornate armchair opposite Carmella, his movements deliberate. "Tensions are good for business," he said, easing himself into the chair. "They keep things spicy, don't you agree?"

"Spicy enough to kill for?" Detective Jones interjected, his tone edged with challenge.

Jason's laugh was sharp, a knife thrown at the insinuation. "Please," he said, waving a hand adorned with a gaudy ring. "Tony's death is a tragedy, sure, but to think I'd dirty my hands over a little rivalry?" His eyes glinted, amused. "You're barking up the wrong tree."

"Then you wouldn't mind telling us—" Carmella began, but Jason cut her off with a dismissive flick of his wrist.

"Baseless accusations," he sneered. "That's all you've brought to my doorstep. And here I thought this might be a visit worth my time."

Detective Jones leaned in, the muscles in his jaw clenching. "Where were you on the night of Tony's murder?" His voice was a low growl, demanding an answer.

Jason tilted his head back slightly, meeting the detective's gaze with a smug lift of his lips. "I was at the annual Flavors Gala," he said, his tone smooth as silk. "Rubbing elbows with the city's culinary elite. Plenty of witnesses to my presence."

The plush carpet muffled their movements as Carmella shifted in her seat, fingers gripping the armrest. She exchanged a quick, frustrated look with Detective Jones. His eyes narrowed for a fleeting moment, a silent acknowledgment of their shared predicament. Without tangible proof to counter Jason's claim, the alibi stood solid as marble.

"Names," Detective Jones pressed, the word sharp as a tack. "We'll need names of these witnesses."

"Of course," Jason replied, a chuckle escaping him as if the request amused him. "You'll find my social circle quite impeccable." He rattled off a list of high-profile individuals, each name dropping like heavy coins into the thickening air of the room.

Carmella's mind churned, skepticism simmering beneath her calm exterior. The scent of expensive cologne mingled with the musty aroma of old books, creating an oppressive atmosphere that seemed to mock their efforts. She knew they were far from cracking Jason's confident facade.

Carmella leaned forward, her gaze sharpening on Jason. "Let's talk about Tony Bianco," she said, her voice threading the air with calm precision. "Your rivalry was no secret in Wavecrest Cove."

Jason's eyes flickered, a muscle twitching in his jaw. He straightened, the smirk melting into a thin line. "Tony?" he scoffed. "Please, it was nothing more than a dance of dough and spice."

"Nothing that would make you want to... remove your competition?" Carmella pressed, watching him closely.

"Absolutely not." Jason's hand swept through the air, a dismissive gesture. Yet, there it was—a spark of heat in those eyes, betraying a momentary lapse from his polished composure. "We simply pushed each other to excel, to be masters of our craft. That's what true chefs do."

"Even if it means stepping on each other's toes?" Carmella kept her tone even, inviting confessions.

"Stepping? Hardly." He chuckled, but it was hollow, edged. "Tony and I, we enjoyed the game. The kitchen is a battlefield, but murder? That's taking it too far." His laugh faded, leaving a silence that clung like cobwebs.

Carmella nodded slowly, processing the shift. She sensed the cracks beneath Jason's confident veneer, the simmering undercurrents of a long-simmered rivalry. But was it enough to boil over into something deadly? The question hung in the air, unanswered.

Carmella's eyes met Detective Jones'. A silent conversation flowed between them, a shared doubt crystallizing in that brief exchange. She leaned back, her fingers drumming softly on the armrest of the velvet chair, while Jones unfolded his arms and pushed off from the bookshelf with a quiet sigh.

"Jason, we appreciate your time," Carmella said, her voice betraying none of the turmoil within.

"Happy to help clear the air," Jason replied, the corner of his mouth twitching upward.

Detective Jones gave a curt nod, his blue eyes scanning the room one last time. "Thank you for your cooperation."

The air in the living room felt heavy as they turned towards the door, each step echoing their unsaid thoughts. They stepped out into the hallway, the door closing behind them with a soft click that seemed to punctuate their departure.

"Another dead end?" Carmella murmured, more to herself than to Jones.

"Seems so," he agreed, the lines of his face set hard with frustration. "But we'll find a lead. We always do."

Their footsteps faded down the corridor, two figures moving through a haze of uncertainty. The plush carpet swallowed the sound of their departure, leaving behind the stillness of a residence—and a resident—shrouded in mystery.

Carmella emerged from the dim corridor into daylight, squinting against the glare of the afternoon sun. The ocean's scent filled her nostrils, the briny tang mingling with the bitter aroma of seaweed. A gull cried overhead, its sharp call a stark contrast to the heavy silence they had left behind.

"Jones," she said, the breeze tugging at her hair. Her gaze locked with his, a spark of resolve flickering within. "Let's go back over what we have. There has to be something we missed."

He looked at her, the sea wind ruffling his dark hair. His eyes, the color of the tumultuous waves beyond, held a silent respect. The corner of his mouth lifted, just barely, in approval.

"Agreed," he responded, his voice firm. "The truth is out there. We just need to find the right thread to pull."

Carmella glanced at her watch. Time was slipping by, each tick a reminder that Tony's killer was still out there. She nodded to Jones. "I'll start with the guest list from the event. Someone must have seen something."

"Good," he grunted. "I'll pull the financials again. Maybe the motive is buried in the books."

They turned away from each other, the decision to split tasks as natural as breathing. Carmella's sneakers scuffed the pavement, her steps brisk and purposeful. The click of Jones's shoes grew fainter, the sound swallowed by the distance between them.

She fished out her phone, thumbing through notes with a frown etched on her face. Each swipe left a trail of fingerprints, smudges over words that held secrets just out of reach. The sun dipped lower, casting long shadows that stretched across Wavecrest Cove like dark fingers.

"Something's there," she whispered to herself. The screen's glow illuminated her determination, a soft halo in the encroaching dusk.

"Keep me posted," Jones called out, his voice carrying over the growing gap.

"Will do," she shouted back, without looking up. Her mind whirred with possibilities, theories knitting together then unraveling just as fast.

They moved apart, solitary figures drawn onward by the gravity of their mission. Carmella's resolve hardened with every step; the truth was a puzzle, and she would piece it together, no matter the cost.

Chapter 12

Carmella shuffled papers on her desk, the office cramped but cozy. Sunlight streamed in through the blinds, casting striped shadows over the evidence spread out like a jigsaw puzzle missing pieces. The scent of tomato sauce and basil from the kitchen below crept up the stairs, mingling with the mustiness of old books.

"Any new thoughts?" Kathleen leaned against the doorframe, arms folded, her green eyes scanning the room.

"Too many," Carmella sighed, tapping a finger on a photo of Tony, his boisterous smile frozen in time. "Something's missing."

"Right in front of us, I bet." Kathleen stepped closer, her red hair catching the light, a fiery contrast to the dimness.

"Tony's pizzeria," Carmella said abruptly, her gaze fixed on a snapshot of Tony's bustling establishment. "We need to go back."

Kathleen raised an eyebrow. "Undercover?"

"Exactly." Carmella stood, resolve hardening her features. "As customers this time."

"Smart." Kathleen nodded. "Less prying eyes."

"Tonight then?" Carmella asked, already planning.

"Tonight." Kathleen confirmed.

They exchanged a look of silent agreement, understanding the risks, the necessity. Determination bound them; they would find the truth hidden within the familiar walls of Wavecrest Cove's culinary battleground.

Carmella pushed open the door to Tony's pizzeria, a bell chiming overhead. Aromas of garlic and yeast enveloped her as she scoped the room, her eyes a beacon of focus. Kathleen slipped in behind, a shadow of grace.

"Table for two?" The hostess's voice cut through the din.

"Corner booth, please," Carmella said, voice even, a practiced smile on her lips.

They slid into the seat, menus untouched. Observant gazes swept over the landscape of diners and servers. An employee joked with regulars, his laugh too loud, movements jerky. Carmella nudged Kathleen, a silent signal.

"Excuse me," Carmella called to the waiter, "Could you tell us about today's specials?"

"Of course," he approached, notepad at the ready. She engaged him, questions light but probing beneath the surface.

Kathleen eased away, unseen in the bustle. She found Tony's office door ajar, the hum of conversation a cover for stealth. Inside, papers cluttered the desk, photos pinned haphazardly to walls.

She rifled through drawers, touch feather-light, green eyes scanning for anomalies. Names, numbers, any thread that might lead back to Otto Marks. Drawers revealed nothing but mundane inventory lists and supplier contacts.

The bookshelf drew her next, an array of cookbooks and business ledgers. Her fingers brushed spines, searching for the click of a latch, the give of a false bottom.

Back in the dining area, Carmella laughed at a story the waiter spun, all the while her gaze never still, missing no detail. She catalogued faces, cross-referencing with the mental list of Tony's known associates.

"Anything good?" Carmella asked when Kathleen returned, slipping into the booth as seamlessly as she'd left.

"Maybe," Kathleen murmured, eyes alight with the thrill of the hunt. "Let's eat and regroup."

"Agreed." Carmella closed her menu, signaling the waiter. They ordered, their mission ongoing, minds churning with possibilities.

Kathleen's fingers paused, a spine out of place. She tugged, heart racing, and a ledger slid free, a hollow behind it. The book was thick, worn at the edges. She flipped it open, and there they were: numbers, dates, names. Otto's scrawled next to Tony's, figures marching in rows. Debt, payment, promises inked in secret.

She reached for her phone, quick snaps of each page. The camera clicked, a silent witness to the hidden dealings. Her hands steady, despite the pulse thrumming in her veins. Evidence gathered, she tucked the ledger back, leaving no trace of her discovery.

In the dining area, Carmella observed, patience her cloak. A man at a corner table caught her eye. His foot tapped a staccato rhythm on the floor, his gaze skittering like leaves in wind. He checked his watch, bit his lip, a portrait of unease.

"Is this seat taken?" Carmella's voice, smooth as cream, broke through his reverie.

"Ah, no," he stuttered, scooting his chair, making room.

"Thank you." She smiled, warmth in her eyes, a balm to his jittery nerves. "I couldn't help but notice you seem a bit... preoccupied. Everything alright?"

"Fine," he said too quickly, then sighed. "Just waiting on someone who's late, is all."

"Ah, I see." Carmella nodded, feigning sympathy. "Busy day, huh? Tony sure knew how to run a tight ship around here." She watched him closely, bait cast.

The man's eyes flickered, caught. "Yeah, Tony... he was good people," he said, voice trailing off, something unsaid hanging between them.

"Was?" Carmella's eyebrow arched, question unvoiced but clear.

"Right, was. Before..." He trailed off again. Carmella leaned in, the scent of tomato sauce and oregano mingling with opportunity.

"Before what happened to him," she finished for him gently, encouraging him to continue.

"Right," he repeated, nodding, words still caged behind his teeth.

Carmella waited, the silence an open door. But the man shook his head, locking away his secrets once more. "I should really get going," he mumbled, standing abruptly.

"Of course," Carmella replied, tone light yet eyes sharp as she watched him flee. Another piece of the puzzle, fluttering just beyond reach.

Carmella's hand rested lightly on the back of the vacant chair, her gaze steady. The nervous customer hesitated, fingers tapping a staccato rhythm on the wooden table. A drop of sweat trailed down his temple, lost in the stubble.

"Actually," he began, voice barely above the din of clinking dishes and murmured conversations, "I did overhear something... unsettling."

"Go on," Carmella urged, her tone even, inviting.

"Tony and Otto..." He swallowed hard, eyes darting to the door as if contemplating escape. "They were here, after hours. Arguing about some deal."

Carmella prompted him with a nod, encouraging the flow of words.

"It was... tense." He wrung his hands. "Otto wanted control—of all three pizzerias. He was pressing Tony, hard."

Kathleen emerged from the shadows, her presence unnoticed until now. Her green eyes locked onto the man, reading his distress.

"Did Tony agree?" she asked sharply.

"Didn't sound like it," the customer replied, a frown creasing his forehead. "Things got heated."

Carmella exchanged a glance with Kathleen, acknowledgment sparking between them. Conspiracies wove through the crust of Wavecrest Cove's serene surface.

"Thank you," Carmella said, her voice firm, reassuring. "You've been very helpful."

The man nodded, relief evident as he slid out of the booth and disappeared into the bustling crowd.

"Otto's been busy," Kathleen observed, tucking a lock of red hair behind her ear.

"Too busy," Carmella agreed, her expressive eyes darkening. "We need to dig deeper. Find out what Otto's really up to."

"Back to 'Nonna's' then," Kathleen decided. "We have some history to unravel."

Silently, they moved towards the exit, their minds already sifting through possibilities, determined to unearth the roots of deceit that threatened their small slice of heaven.

The door to "Nonna's Slice of Heaven" chimed softly as Carmella and Kathleen stepped into the familiar warmth of the pizzeria. Tables lay vacant, save for a few scattered crumbs from the day's hustle. The scent of tomato and basil lingered in the air, a comforting blanket that now shrouded their meticulous task.

"Let's start with the archives," Kathleen murmured, pulling her laptop from her bag. Her fingers danced across the keys, green eyes focused and searching.

Carmella nodded, flipping through a stack of old town records and newspapers they'd gathered. Dust motes floated lazily in the beam of sunlight streaming through the window. Each page turn was a whisper, a step back through history, a breadcrumb on the trail they hoped would lead to the truth.

Hours ticked by, marked only by the rhythmic tapping of keys and the soft rustling of paper. A half-drunk cup of coffee grew cold next to Carmella, forgotten in her absorption.

"Look at this," Kathleen's voice sliced through the silence. She angled the screen so Carmella could see an old newspaper article, yellowed and brittle with age. The headline screamed of a dispute, a feud between families, rooted deep in Wavecrest Cove's past.

"Otto and Tony's grandparents," Carmella read aloud, her brow furrowing. "A rivalry over recipes and territory?"

"Seems like it." Kathleen zoomed in on a black-and-white photo of two stern-faced men, standing rigidly apart. "Their bad blood goes way back."

Carmella leaned closer, studying the photograph. The same stubborn set to the jaw, the same piercing gaze—traits that had trickled down through generations. "Could Otto have held onto that grudge all these years?"

"Maybe never let it go," Kathleen said, tracing a line of text on the screen. "It says here their competition almost split the town in two."

"Old feuds die hard," Carmella mused. She stood up, stretching her cramped muscles. "This could be the motive we've been missing. Otto didn't just want control; he wanted vengeance."

"Vengeance served cold," Kathleen agreed, shutting the laptop with a decisive click. "And it looks like Tony paid the price."

Together, they contemplated the gravity of their discovery. History had cast a long shadow over Wavecrest Cove, and now they stood at the edge of its darkness, ready to chase the truth wherever it led.

"Concrete evidence," Carmella said, tapping her finger against the tabletop. "That's what we need."

Kathleen nodded, her green eyes scanning the empty café. "Witnesses," she replied. "Someone must have seen something."

They rose from their seats in sync, a silent agreement passing between them. The bell above the door jingled as they stepped into the cool evening air of Wavecrest Cove.

"Let's hit the bar," Carmella suggested, her voice carrying an edge of urgency. "It's where secrets spill as easily as beer."

"Right behind you," Kathleen said, her tall frame casting long shadows on the pavement.

The local bar was dim, the clinking of glasses and muffled conversations wrapping around them like fog. They moved through the crowd, two predators hunting in a forest of denim and flannel.

"Act natural," Kathleen murmured, her red hair a beacon in the low light.

Carmella ordered drinks, her casual banter with the bartender masking her scrutiny of the patrons. Kathleen leaned against the bar, eyes flitting across the room, alert for any sign of recognition or guilt.

"See that?" Carmella whispered, nodding subtly toward a group of pizzeria workers huddled at a corner table.

"Could be nothing," Kathleen replied. "Or everything."

They sipped their drinks, the bitter tang of hops sharp on their tongues. Time stretched thin as they waited, watched, and listened.

"Listen," a voice slurred nearby. "Otto... he was there that night. Saw him with my own eyes."

Carmella's heartbeat quickened; she exchanged a glance with Kathleen. This was it—a lead, fragile but vital.

"Who was there?" Carmella asked, feigning curiosity as she sidled closer to the source of the overheard snippet.

"Otto Marks," the man said, his words heavy with alcohol and importance. "Arguing with Tony outside the back door. I saw 'em."

"Did anyone else see this?" Kathleen chimed in, her tone light but insistent.

"Can't say," the man shrugged, his attention waning. "But I heard things."

"Thank you," Carmella said, her smile a mask. They had a thread to follow, one that could unravel Otto's carefully woven lies.

"Let's go," Kathleen said softly, touching Carmella's arm. "We've got work to do."

They left the warmth of the bar, the night air sobering. The pieces were coming together, and with each step, they drew closer to the truth.

The bell above the bar door jingled as Carmella and Kathleen stepped out into the bracing night. They pulled their jackets tighter against the chill, a shiver running down their spines that wasn't entirely from the cold. The hours had worn on, voices blending into a cacophony of near-misses and dead ends until one clear note had risen above the rest.

"Otto Marks?" The name had tumbled out of a weary dishwasher's mouth, his eyes bloodshot but certain. "Yeah, saw him. He had this big ol' duffel bag, looked heavy. Left out back, right after his shouting match with Tony."

"Would you be willing to tell that to the authorities?" Kathleen's voice held a careful blend of hope and gravity.

"Sure," the man nodded, draining his glass. "Tony was good people. Didn't deserve what happened."

Back at Nonna's Slice of Heaven, they huddled in Carmella's cramped office. Papers, photos, and notes sprawled across the desk like a roadmap of their journey so far. The ledger's digital images glowed from the laptop screen—numbers and dates whispering secrets. Kathleen tapped her fingers on the tabletop, energy coursing through her.

"Okay, we've got a witness," she said, voice low with resolve. "And evidence. It's time, Carmella."

"Time," Carmella echoed. Her mind raced, thoughts sharp and focused. She thought about the legacy of her family, their reputation woven into the fabric of Wavecrest Cove. This was more than just a mission to find the truth; it was a stand for justice, for community, for Tony.

"Otto won't know what hit him," Carmella stated, her expressive eyes fierce in the lamplight. She reached for the folder containing the witness statement, its contents heavier than paper and ink.

"Right." Kathleen's green eyes gleamed. "We'll need to be strategic. He's cunning, but we've got the upper hand now."

"Tomorrow," Carmella decided. "First thing. We confront Otto Marks."

"Agreed." Kathleen stood, stretching out her tall frame. "Rest up. Tomorrow we end this."

They shared a nod, each lost briefly in their own determination, before turning out the lights and locking up. The quiet streets of Wavecrest Cove lay before them, holding its breath for the dawn of confrontation.

The bell above the door jangled sharply as Carmella pushed it open, the scent of baking dough and melted cheese instantly enveloping her. Kathleen followed close behind, her gaze sweeping over the familiar checkered tablecloths and faux grapevines twining around rustic beams. Otto's pizzeria, usually a place of comfort, now held an undercurrent of danger.

Mama Mia It's Murder

"Carmella, Kathleen," Otto greeted, his voice devoid of warmth. Thin glasses perched on his nose, he looked up from wiping down the counter with a white cloth. His blue eyes met theirs, betraying no hint of the storm that was about to break.

"Otto," Carmella replied, her tone even. "We need to talk."

"Indeed?" Otto raised an eyebrow, setting the cloth aside with deliberate care. "Then talk."

"Privately," Kathleen insisted, her voice steady.

Otto considered for a moment, then nodded curtly towards his office. The three of them threaded through tables, past the clinking of cutlery and murmur of conversations. Behind the closed office door, the outside world fell away, leaving only the ticking of a clock.

"Sit," Otto commanded, gesturing to the chairs before his desk.

They remained standing, a united front. Carmella's hand gripped the folder, her knuckles white. Otto settled into his chair, steepling his fingers and eyeing them over the top.

"Let's skip pleasantries," Carmella said. "We know what you did."

"Accusations require proof," Otto replied, his voice smooth.

"Here's your proof." Kathleen slapped the photos of the hidden ledger on the desk. They landed with a slap, loud in the hushed room.

"And we have a witness." Carmella's words sliced the air.

Otto's eyes flicked to the photos, then back to Carmella. He leaned back, the creak of leather loud in the silence.

"Your move, Mr. Marks," Kathleen said.

Otto's mouth twitched, a mere ghost of a smile. "You think you have me cornered."

"We do," Carmella affirmed, her heart pounding.

"Perhaps." Otto's gaze cooled. "But I'd advise caution. Accusations can be... messy."

"Justice often is," Carmella countered.

"Justice," Otto mused. "An intriguing concept."

"Confess, Otto," Kathleen urged. "It's over."

"Is it?" Otto's eyes locked onto Carmella's. "I wonder..."

"Tony deserves the truth," Carmella said, her voice unyielding.

"Tony..." Otto trailed off, his expression unreadable.

"Wavecrest Cove deserves better than a murderer serving slices," Carmella declared.

"Perhaps." Otto stood, the chair scraping back. He circled the desk slowly, facing them. "But remember, every story has two sides."

"Only one side is the truth," Kathleen retorted.

Otto paused, inches from them. A tense silence spread, thick as the sauce on his pizzas.

"Consider your next step carefully, ladies," Otto whispered.

"Justice isn't a step," Carmella replied. "It's a leap. And we're ready to jump."

Otto's eyes narrowed. The game was on.

Chapter 13

Carmella pushed open the heavy wooden door of the Wavecrest Cove Historical Society. The scent of must and old paper wafted toward her, mingling with the faint lemon tang of furniture polish. She glanced back at Kathleen, her eyes narrowing with determination.

"Ready to dig up some dirt on Otto?" Carmella asked.

"Always," Kathleen replied, a spark of mischief in her green eyes. Her red hair seemed to shimmer under the fluorescent lights as they stepped into the quiet repository of the town's history.

The two women moved through aisles lined with bookshelves and filing cabinets, their hands brushing against the spines of leather-bound volumes and stacks of yellowing documents. They reached the archives, where a large table awaited them, bare except for the soft glow of a solitary desk lamp.

Kathleen pulled out a chair and sat down, her long legs folding gracefully beneath the table. "Let's start with the newspapers. If Otto's been up to no good, it's bound to be in print somewhere."

Carmella nodded and reached for a stack of microfiche reels, loading one into the reader. The machine hummed to life, casting an eerie blue light over her petite frame. She peered into the viewer, her brow furrowing as she scanned the headlines.

"Got something," Carmella murmured a few minutes later. She adjusted the focus, revealing an article dated several years back. "Listen to this—'Otto Marks: Culinary Conqueror or Cutthroat Competitor?'"

"Sounds juicy," Kathleen quipped, leaning forward to get a better look.

Carmella read aloud, her voice steady but laced with incredulity. "Local pizzeria owner Otto Marks is well-known for his high-quality pies, but rumors swirl about the aggressive tactics he employs to maintain his hold on the market..."

"Aggressive tactics?" Kathleen echoed, tilting her head. "Oh, this is just what we need."

"Here's more," Carmella continued. "Multiple anonymous sources have hinted at intimidation, sabotage, and even threats being used to shut down anyone who dares challenge the pizza king of Wavecrest Cove."

"Intimidation? That's our Otto alright," Kathleen said, her tone dry.

"Look at this." Carmella pointed to a grainy black-and-white photo accompanying the article. It showed a younger Otto, stern-faced, standing outside his establishment, arms crossed defiantly over his chest. "He's always had that look—like he's guarding secrets."

"Or guarding his empire," Kathleen added. "We've got to find more. This is just the tip of the iceberg."

Carmella nodded, her wavy brown hair bouncing slightly as she loaded another reel. The room filled with the soft clicks and whirrs of the microfiche reader, punctuated by the occasional rustle of paper as they unearthed further evidence of Otto's ruthless reputation.

"Wavecrest Cove may seem tranquil," Carmella said, half to herself, "but beneath the surface, there's a war being waged—one slice at a time."

Carmella's fingers danced across her notepad, scribbling furiously as the former dough tosser spilled his truths. "He had eyes everywhere," the man muttered, glancing over his shoulder. "Otto didn't just want to win; he wanted everyone else to lose."

"Everyone else?" Kathleen prodded, her voice a mix of intrigue and disbelief.

"Every last one," he confirmed, his hands trembling slightly. "If another pizza joint got a good review or a new topping became popular, Otto would be on it—squashing it before it could flourish."

The next interviewee, a waitress with tired eyes, recounted evenings spent watching Otto pace the floor of his pizzeria after hours. "He'd make calls, lots of them," she whispered. "Always talking about 'protecting the turf' and 'keeping the family fed.' But there was no warmth in it. It was all cold strategy."

"Thank you," Carmella said softly, offering a smile that held more sadness than gratitude. They left the woman with a nod, her story echoing in their ears.

In the basement of the historical society, dust motes floated in the slivers of light that pierced the gloom. Shelves groaned under the weight of forgotten lore. Carmella led the way, her petite frame weaving between stacks of aging tomes and artifacts.

"Over here," Kathleen called out. A door, previously obscured by a tall filing cabinet, revealed itself at her insistence. The lock gave in with a satisfying click, surrendering its secrets to their search.

Inside, time stood still. Stacks of documents towered like ancient sentinels. Photographs, sepia-toned and curling at the edges, lay scattered among ledgers thick with entries in faded ink.

"Look at this," Carmella murmured, pulling out a photo. Not the one of Otto with influential figures—that one remained hidden—but an image of a young Otto standing beside a brick oven, the fire within casting shadows over his determined face.

Kathleen unearthed an envelope, heavy with contents. She drew out the papers, eyes scanning rapidly. "These are property deeds," she said, her breath catching. "And look..." Her finger traced a line of text. "...signed over under duress."

"Coercion? Blackmail?" Carmella suggested, her mind racing with the implications.

"Or worse," Kathleen added, her voice a whisper as she replaced the documents with reverent care.

The air grew colder, the silence deeper. With each discovery, the picture of Otto Marks, the unassuming pizzeria owner with an iron fist, became clearer, more sinister. Carmella felt the chill of reality seep into her bones: Wavecrest Cove's pizza king was a tyrant in disguise, and they were closer than ever to unraveling his reign.

Carmella's fingers brushed over the dusty frames, her heart quickening. A particular photo caught her eye—a black and white snapshot that sang of bygone eras. There was Otto, no hint of gray in his hair, flanked by men whose faces bore the stamp of influence: a mayor, a judge, a well-known entrepreneur. Power radiated from the stiff pose, a silent testament to connections woven deep into Wavecrest Cove's fabric.

"Kathleen, look." Carmella's voice barely rose above a whisper, yet it cut through the stillness like a knife. "He wasn't alone in this."

Kathleen peered over Carmella's shoulder, her green eyes narrowing. "Allies in high places," she murmured. "It figures."

The revelation hung between them, heavy as the air itself.

Across the room, Kathleen shuffled through a stack of letters, her movements methodical. She paused, drawing out a cream-colored envelope with a jagged tear at the corner. Inside, a series of typed letters lay flat and unassuming. But their words...

"Listen to this." Kathleen's tone hardened, her usual humor gone. "'Consider this your final warning,'" she read aloud. The threat in the sentence slithered across the floorboards. "'Your doors stay open at your peril.'"

Carmella sucked in a sharp breath. "He wrote that?"

"Signed, sealed, and delivered." Kathleen flipped through more letters, each one echoing the last in malice. "There's a whole pile of them. He terrorized the competition."

"Without mercy," Carmella added, her thoughts churning. Otto's ambition was not just a drive; it was a weapon, honed and ready to strike at the heart of anyone who dared to challenge him.

As Kathleen set the letters aside, the two women exchanged a look that transcended words. They were on the right track, but the path ahead bristled with the thorns of Otto's dark past. Together, they would need to tread carefully, for the truth they sought was guarded by a man who played a very dangerous game.

Carmella spread out the newspaper clippings across the table, each headline a breadcrumb leading further into Otto's shadowy ascent. Her finger traced the timeline, from the opening of his first pizzeria to the abrupt demise of his last known rival. Notes and dates mingled, forming a pattern as clear as the constellations above Wavecrest Cove.

"Look at this," she said, tapping an article dated five years prior. "The same month Giordano's shut down, Otto launched his second location—right across the street."

Kathleen leaned in, her green eyes scanning the text. "He was always two steps ahead," she murmured, her voice low with realization.

"Or he made sure everyone else was two steps behind," Carmella countered, her brows knitting together.

A creak echoed through the room as Kathleen pulled open a rusty file cabinet. Dust motes danced in the slanting light, disturbed from their resting place. She drew out a leather-bound diary, worn at the edges, and gently cracked it open.

"Listen to this," Kathleen whispered, her voice a thread of sound against the stillness. "It's from Leo Rossi, Otto's old partner. 'I fear I've seen too much, witnessed the lengths to which Otto will go. My sleep is fitful, haunted by the thought that my days as a free man are numbered.'"

Carmella's pulse quickened, her skin prickling with a mix of dread and determination. Otto had not just built an empire—he had erected a fortress, stone by ruthless stone.

"Does it say what he saw?" Carmella asked, leaning closer.

"Nothing specific." Kathleen flipped through the pages, her fingers careful not to crumble the aging paper. "But there's fear in every entry. The kind that eats at you."

"Enough to make a man disappear," Carmella concluded, her voice barely above a whisper.

The two friends shared a glance, the weight of discovery pressing upon them. Otto's past was a tapestry woven with intimidation and silence. But Carmella knew, with Kathleen by her side, they would unravel it thread by thread.

Carmella's hand trembled as she reached for a manila envelope marked 'Confidential.' Inside, photographs depicted various pizzerias around Wavecrest Cove—some thriving, others shuttered with boards. Her thumb paused on a grainy image of a shifty-eyed man slipping something into a crate of mozzarella.

"Kathleen, look at this," Carmella said, spreading the photos across the table.

"Isn't that Jerry Smith? Works for the health department?" Kathleen squinted at the picture, recognition flashing in her eyes.

"Caught red-handed," Carmella muttered. The scent of mildew from the old documents filled her nostrils as she sifted through more pictures, each one adding depth to the sinister puzzle.

"Here's something." Kathleen held up a stack of papers, her voice steady despite the bombshell they were about to drop. "Letters between Otto and Jerry. They're talking codes, dates, places... It's a sabotage schedule."

"Let me see." Carmella snatched the sheets, scanning the words rapidly. Otto's handwriting was meticulous, the loops and lines betraying no hint of his malicious intent. Jerry's replies were just as calculated, their professional veneer thinly veiling the corruption beneath.

"Otto had him in his pocket," Carmella concluded, her lips a tight line. She could almost hear the clink of money changing hands, the quiet whispers of conspiracy.

"Explains why no one could pin anything on him," Kathleen added, her fingers drumming against the wooden tabletop. "He knew how to play the game too well."

"Too well," Carmella echoed. The room seemed to close in on them, walls steeped in the history of Otto's deceit. They had unearthed the truth, now they needed to bring it to light.

"Let's get this evidence to the right hands," Kathleen said, resolve hardening her features. "It's time Otto played by the rules."

"Agreed." Carmella gathered the damning documents, feeling the weight of justice in her grasp. Otto's empire was built on lies, but the truth was a powerful weapon, and she intended to wield it with precision.

The door creaked, a soft groan in the dimly lit corridor. Carmella's fingers were tense around the evidence, her knuckles white. Kathleen strode ahead, her green eyes scanning the shadows for their quarry. They found him hunched over a desk piled with dusty ledgers, the glow of a solitary desk lamp carving deep lines into his weary face.

"Michael," Kathleen's voice cut through the quiet, "we need to talk."

He straightened, the chair squealing a protest. His gaze darted between the two women, apprehension written plain on his features.

"About Otto?" he whispered, as if even saying the name could invoke trouble.

"Yes," Carmella stepped forward, her heart hammering against her ribs. "We know what he made you do."

Michael's hands shook, the truth unspooling in the tremors that seized his fingers. He wiped his brow, sweat beading despite the chill in the room.

"He threatened my family," Michael confessed, eyes downcast. "I had no choice."

"Tell us everything." Kathleen's command was gentle but firm, her presence an anchor in the storm of Michael's fear.

He recounted tales of tampered dough mixtures, midnight visits to rival pizzerias, and whispered warnings that turned into screams in the dark. Otto's shadow loomed large in every word, a puppeteer of malice pulling strings behind the scenes.

"Thank you, Michael." Carmella's gratitude was sincere, a balm to the man's frayed nerves. She exchanged a glance with Kathleen, resolve hardening in her core.

They left the historical society with determination etching their paths. The sun dipped low, casting long shadows across Wavecrest Cove. Otto's restaurant stood at the end of the street, windows aglow with false warmth.

"Ready?" Carmella asked, her voice steadier than she felt.

"Let's take him down," Kathleen replied, her stride purposeful.

They approached the entrance, evidence clutched like a shield. Otto Marks' reign over Wavecrest Cove's pizza scene was about to crumble, piece by incriminating piece. Justice for Tony was within reach, and Carmella and Kathleen were its harbingers.

Chapter 14

The bell above the pizzeria's back door jingled, a quaint sound out of place with the gravity of the moment. Carmella pushed into the dimly lit room, her petite frame rigid, a folder of papers clutched in her hands like a shield. Beside her, Kathleen's shadow stretched long across the flour-dusted floor, her posture tall and unyielding.

"Otto," Carmella said, her voice slicing the musty air of tomato sauce and baked dough. She laid the folder on the stainless-steel prep table with a soft slap.

Otto turned from the brick oven, a peel still in hand. His blue eyes met theirs over thin-rimmed glasses, his expression unreadable. "Ladies," he greeted, the corner of his mouth twitching upward.

"We've found something," Kathleen stated, her voice level, her gaze never leaving Otto's face. "Evidence."

"Against you," Carmella added, pushing the folder towards him.

"Have you now?" Otto set down the peel, wiping his hands on his apron with deliberate slowness. He didn't reach for the folder.

"Tony's death wasn't an accident," Kathleen continued. Her words hung between them, a challenge.

"Is that what you think?" Otto's laugh was a low chuckle, devoid of warmth. He leaned back against the counter, arms crossed. "Baseless accusations."

Carmella's breath hitched, but she held his stare. "Not baseless. We know—"

"Know? You know nothing," Otto interrupted, his calm tone a stark contrast to the tension in the room. "Speculation. Conjecture."

"Look at the evidence," Carmella insisted, flicking the folder open with a finger. Photographs and notes glared up at Otto, silent accusers.

"Girls playing detective," Otto said, amusement threading through his words. "But this is real life, not a game."

Kathleen's lips pressed into a thin line, her green eyes sharp. "We're not playing."

"Nor am I," Otto retorted smoothly. The amusement had fallen away, leaving behind the hard edge of reality.

Carmella's cheeks flared a heated red, the muscles in her jaw tensing. "My grandfather built something beautiful here," she said, her voice climbing with each word. "You can't just sweep his legacy under the rug like it's nothing."

Otto remained unmoved, a statue carved from ice. "Accidents happen," he replied, his voice a monotone.

"Accidents?" Carmella's hands balled into fists at her sides, the paper of the evidence crinkling beneath her grip. "You expect us to believe that? After everything we've found?"

"Believe what you will," Otto said, shrugging one shoulder as if the matter were trifling.

Kathleen stepped closer, her eyes narrowing. "Your alibi," she began, her tone laced with incredulity, "it's full of holes." She leaned in, her height casting a shadow over Otto. "You said you closed up shop early that night, but the time stamp on the security footage from across the street says otherwise."

Otto's lips pressed together for a brief moment, betraying a crack in his armor. "Cameras can be faulty," he countered, regaining his composure.

"Faulty?" Kathleen's laugh was sharp, a shard of glass. "Or inconvenient for you?"

"Speculation isn't evidence," Otto stated flatly.

Carmella stepped forward, her resolve hardened. "We're not leaving until we get the truth," she declared, her voice steady despite the pounding of her heart.

Otto met her gaze, his own eyes cold and calculating. The game had changed; no more dismissive chuckles. Now there was only the silent battle of wills.

"Truth is a matter of perspective," he said at last.

"Then let's hear yours," Kathleen challenged, unblinking.

The room thrummed with tension, the scent of tomato sauce and yeast heavy in the air. Carmella's breath came fast, her determination a palpable force. Otto faced them, an enigma, his next words poised to tip the scales.

Otto shifted, a muscle twitching in his jaw. His eyes, once veiled in disinterest, narrowed—a glint of annoyance breaking through. "Ladies," he began, his tone taking on a note of condescension, "you're barking up the wrong tree."

"Really?" Kathleen's voice was dry as old parchment.

"Indeed." He straightened, the ghost of a smirk tugging at his lips. "Perhaps you've overlooked young Ricky from the grocery store? A troubled lad, always loitering around after hours."

Carmella's pulse quickened, but she didn't miss a beat. "Ricky has an alibi," she retorted, her words slicing the air between them. "He was working that night. The manager confirmed it."

"Managers can be... persuaded," Otto suggested, his eyes darting between the two women, gauging their reactions.

"Stop deflecting." Carmella's stance was solid, her voice a steady drumbeat against his evasions. "We've checked. We've double-checked. You're the one with something to hide."

"Am I?" Otto leaned back against the stainless steel prep table, arms folded over his chest. "Or is this just a witch hunt?"

"Your delivery van was there, Otto." Carmella stepped closer, her gaze never faltering. "At Tony's place. The night he died."

"Coincidences happen," he murmured, but the flicker of doubt had crept into his eyes.

"Too many coincidences make a pattern," Carmella said, her voice firm. She held his gaze, searching for the telltale signs of a lie. "We'll find the truth."

Otto's mouth tightened, the mask of control slipping. "We shall see," he said, but the tremor in his voice betrayed him. They were closer to the truth than he wanted to admit.

The room was a battleground of wills, the scent of tomato sauce and yeast hanging heavy like the unspoken words between them. Carmella's hands were fists at her sides, every muscle in her body coiled tight with resolve. Kathleen's shadow stretched long across the checkered floor, her posture straight as an arrow, eyes sharp and piercing.

"Really now," Otto began, his voice smooth as the marble countertop, "Aren't you two a bit too close to see clearly? Friendship can blind you to the facts."

"Nice try," Kathleen cut in, her tone sharper than the pizza cutter on the wall. "But we're not here to play games."

"Of course not," Otto said, tilting his head slightly. "But consider this—perhaps Carmella wants to find a scapegoat to save her family's name, no matter the cost." His gaze shifted to Carmella, speculative. "Even if it means suspecting an innocent man."

Carmella's eyes blazed, the accusation hitting its mark, but she did not waver. "My grandfather built his life on honesty, not deceit. That's more than I can say for some."

Otto's lips twitched. "And Kathleen," he continued, turning towards her, "Isn't it convenient to stand by your friend? The librarian and the pizzeria heiress—quite the story. But what about objectivity?"

"Your insinuations are pathetic," Kathleen retorted, her words slicing through the tension. "We've got evidence, not just theories."

"Alleged evidence," Otto corrected smoothly, eyeing them both. "Circumstantial at best."

"Enough," Carmella's voice cracked like a whip. "You won't tear us apart with doubt. We know what we found."

Otto's expression hardened, a crack in his composure. He took a slow breath, the calm before the storm. "We'll see."

Carmella stiffened, the jab at her loyalty a sharp thorn. She turned to Kathleen. Time slowed as their gazes locked—a silent exchange in a glance. No words needed, the message clear: trust unbroken. They stood side by side, an unbreakable unit against Otto's ploys.

"Divide and conquer?" Carmella's voice held a hint of mockery, belying the steel beneath. "Not today, Otto."

Kathleen smirked, arms folded. "Try harder."

Otto's jaw clenched. The air in the cramped back room grew colder, denser. He leaned forward, his hands flat on the stainless-steel prep table. His blue eyes, once cool pools, now blazed with a fire that had lurked beneath his calm exterior.

"Listen carefully," he began, voice barely above a whisper yet slicing through the silence like a blade. "You're playing with fire, and you will get burned."

Carmella's heart raced, but she stood rooted, defiant. Kathleen's breath hitched imperceptibly—only a friend would notice.

"Is that a threat?" Kathleen's question was pointed, her stance ready for battle.

"Take it as... advice." The menace in Otto's tone wrapped around them, a serpent coiling for the strike.

"Your 'advice' falls on deaf ears," Carmella retorted. Her body tensed, prepared for whatever came next. Otto's threats couldn't sway them; they were in this together until the end.

Carmella squared her shoulders, her eyes never leaving Otto's. "Threats won't work," she said, her voice a solid beam of resolve. She stepped closer, the scent of tomato sauce and oregano in the air giving way to the electric tang of tension. "The truth has a way of coming out. Justice will have its day."

Otto scoffed, but his posture betrayed him; a hint of uncertainty crept into his stance. The fluorescent lights hummed overhead, casting stark shadows across their faces. Kathleen shifted beside Carmella, her silence a stalwart echo of support.

"Justice?" Otto's lips twisted into a sardonic smile. "A pretty notion."

"More than a notion," Kathleen interjected sharply. "A promise."

The room seemed to contract, the walls pressing in as if bearing witness to the standoff. Each breath sounded loud in the hush, each shift of weight a pronouncement. Otto studied them, the cogs turning behind calculating eyes.

"You'll find that promises can be broken," he said, voice laced with a warning as thin as the crust on his pizzas.

"Maybe," Carmella replied, her gaze unyielding. "But not by you."

Otto's eyes flickered. He opened his mouth, then closed it, the grip of inevitability tightening around the room. He looked from Carmella to Kathleen and back, the play of emotions across his face a silent symphony of realization and defeat.

"Mark my words," he finally said, a gravelly undertone of desperation threading through his speech. "You don't know what you're stirring up."

"We know enough," Carmella said. Her pulse thrummed in her ears, syncopated with the ticking of the wall clock—the countdown to the moment of truth.

"Enough to take you down," Kathleen added, her words crisp, leaving no room for ambiguity.

Otto's next move was anybody's guess. Would he confess, lash out, or continue to weave his web of deceit? The air vibrated with the weight of unspoken truths, ready to shatter the fragile veneer of the pizzeria's back room.

"Be careful, girls," Otto warned, a low growl. "Some truths are better left buried."

"Then you should have thought twice before burying them," Carmella countered.

Kathleen nodded, her emerald eyes glinting with the same unbreakable spirit that kept Carmella anchored. They stood united, two against one, at the edge of revelation. Whatever came next, they were ready.

Chapter 15

Carmella slumped into the faded cushions of her grandmother's floral sofa, the fabric threadbare from decades of comfort-seeking visitors to 'Nonna's Slice of Heaven.' Her fingers drummed a defeated rhythm on the wooden armrest. Across the room, Kathleen mirrored her posture, elbows on knees, head cradled in her hands. The air between them hung thick with the weight of unsolved mysteries and unspoken worry.

"Maybe we're missing something obvious," Carmella whispered, more to herself than to Kathleen. It was an attempt to reignite the spark. To push back against the creeping doubt that they might never find the answers they sought.

"Or maybe the entire town is in on it," Kathleen muttered, her voice laced with sarcasm born of frustration rather than humor. A wry smile touched the corners of her mouth, though her green eyes remained clouded with concern.

The silence stretched on, marked only by the ticking of the antique clock on the mantelpiece. It was a relentless reminder that time, much like their investigation, marched forward with or without their consent.

Then, piercing the stillness, Kathleen's phone erupted with the shrill chime of a notification. The sound jolted them both, breaking the tension as effectively as a crack of thunder shatters the calm before a storm. They exchanged looks, the shift in their expressions palpable. Despair gave way to curiosity, hope flickering in their eyes like candlelight challenging the dark.

"Could be another dead-end," Carmella cautioned, but her tone betrayed her eagerness for any lead that might pull them from this investigative quagmire.

"Only one way to find out," Kathleen replied, her thumb hovering over the glowing screen. She tapped, unlocking the potential promise held within that small electronic herald.

Kathleen's fingers trembled slightly as she tapped the screen, enlarging the text of the message that had arrived unannounced into their evening of dead ends. She cleared her throat, a soft prelude to the revelation they both hoped would turn the tide in their favor.

"When the moon shines bright," Kathleen began, her voice steady now, "follow the scent of basil to find the truth."

A hush fell over the room, the cryptic words hanging in the air like mist. Carmella leaned forward, elbows on knees, her mind racing to decode the riddle that had been cast into their lap. It was a beacon in the gloom, an enigmatic signpost pointing toward hope or perhaps another disappointment. Yet it was all they had.

"Fresh basil," Carmella murmured, more to herself than Kathleen. Her eyes, bright with sudden understanding, snapped up. "Otto Marks."

"Otto?" Kathleen echoed, her brow knitting in confusion before realization dawned. "The pizzeria?"

"Always fresh basil in his sauce," Carmella affirmed with a nod, her petite frame straightening as resolve coursed through her veins. Otto's dedication to his culinary craft was well-known, but now it seemed there might be more to his herb of choice than mere flavor.

"Could it be that simple?" Kathleen wondered aloud, skepticism threading her words. Yet the possibility dangled before them, too enticing to ignore.

"Only one way to find out," Carmella said, rising from her chair with newfound determination etched in her features. The game was afoot once more, and this time, they had a direction to follow.

Carmella seized her keys from the coffee table. The metallic jangle cut through the stillness of the room as she turned to Kathleen, her partner in amateur sleuthing. "Let's go," she said, her voice a mix of command and excitement.

Kathleen nodded, her green eyes reflecting the urgency. They both knew that clues like these didn't come with the luxury of time. The two women hurried out of Carmella's living room, the door closing behind them with a resolute click.

They descended the porch steps in tandem, the evening chill wrapping around them like an unwelcome shawl. The town of Wavecrest Cove slept around them, its quaint charm veiled in the darkness of night. Only one goal illuminated their path: Otto's pizzeria.

"Think he's there now?" Kathleen asked between breaths, her curiosity never waning despite the brisk pace they maintained.

"Doesn't matter. We have to check it out," Carmella replied, her sneakers thudding against the sidewalk. She had always been decisive, a trait honed from her New York days, but now it was fueled by the weight of the mystery at hand.

As they neared the commercial district where Otto's establishment stood like a sentinel, the moon revealed itself from behind a cloak of scudding clouds. It bathed the quiet streets in silver, making the mundane seem otherworldly.

"Look at that moon," Kathleen murmured, her gaze lifting.

"Full and bright," Carmella echoed, her own eyes drawn upward. The moon's glow seemed to endorse their mission, guiding them forward.

"Feels like it's watching over us," Kathleen added, the corners of her mouth lifting slightly. Even in the gravity of their task, her wit found a way to surface.

"Or leading the way," Carmella countered, a smile tugging at the edges of her lips despite the tension knotting her stomach.

The pair quickened their stride as Otto's pizzeria came into view, its sign darkened, the usual bustle of patrons absent. The moon hung overhead, a silent guardian in the velvet tapestry of the night sky. A sense of anticipation tinged with fear gripped them. Every step brought them closer to answers or potential danger. But the truth lay hidden within those walls, under the watchful eye of the moon, and they were ready to uncover it.

The door to Otto's pizzeria creaked open with a gentle push from Carmella's hand. A waft of basil, potent and distinct, greeted them like an old friend with secrets to spill. Carmella inhaled the familiar aroma, her pulse quickening. The scent was more than just an ingredient here; it was a signpost.

"Smell that?" she whispered to Kathleen, who nodded, her eyes alert and scanning.

"Fresh basil... Otto's special touch," Kathleen replied, her voice barely above a hush.

They tiptoed across the checkered floor, avoiding the patches of moonlight streaming through the windows. They moved as shadows, slipping past rows of empty tables towards the kitchen. Pots and pans hung silent above their heads, bearing witness to their careful intrusion.

Carmella gestured towards the stainless-steel countertops, gleaming dully in the low light. Together, they sifted through drawers filled with utensils and recipe cards. Nothing. They shifted their attention to the storage area, where stacks of boxes towered like city skylines.

"Here, help me with this," Carmella said, tugging at a shelf laden with cans of tomato sauce. They repositioned it, revealing nothing but dust bunnies dancing in its wake.

"Let's try the office," Kathleen suggested, her brow furrowed with determination.

Carmella followed, her sneakers silent on the tiled floor. The office was cramped, papers strewn across the desk, a testament to hurried workdays and long nights. They rifled through invoices, their fingers nimble and searching. Receipts fluttered to the floor, photographs slipped between their fingers, each a potential piece of the puzzle.

"Anything?" Carmella asked, hope threading through her words.

"Still looking," Kathleen responded, her tone resolute.

They continued their search, meticulous and thorough, leaving the office as their last stone unturned. Every corner held the promise of revelation, every paper a possible lead. The moon outside cast long shadows, painting their investigation with strokes of urgency.

"Keep going," Carmella urged, her gaze locked on the task. "We're on to something. I can feel it."

Kathleen nodded, mirroring Carmella's resolve. They worked in tandem, fueled by instinct and the quiet strength that had brought them this far. The night grew older, but their spirits did not wane. They were close, closer than ever to the truth that had eluded them. And under the watchful eye of the moon, they pressed on.

Kathleen's fingers traced the grain of the wooden shelf, her touch light and searching. A faint line appeared, almost imperceptible against the dark varnish. She paused, leaned closer. "Carmella, look."

Carmella edged nearer, her own hands hesitant as they hovered over Kathleen's discovery. The shelf didn't belong, an afterthought against the storeroom's practicality. They exchanged a glance, a silent agreement passing between them.

"Help me with this," Kathleen whispered, her voice barely rising above a breath.

Together, they nudged at the shelf. It shifted, a soft click sounding from the wall. The compartment revealed itself, cleverly concealed but now exposed to their keen observation. Hope sparked in Carmella's chest, quick and bright.

"Got it." Carmella's voice held reverence, as if acknowledging the gravity of their find.

The compartment door swung open with a creak of reluctance. Inside, amidst the shadows, lay a stack of papers. Carmella reached in, her fingers steady despite the adrenaline that thrummed through her veins. Invoices topped the pile, crisp and formal. Receipts followed, their edges worn from handling. Photographs slipped between the layers, faces and places captured in still life.

"Start sorting," Carmella instructed, her words clipped with urgency.

They worked, the silence around them dense, punctuated only by the shuffle of paper and the occasional sharp intake of breath as pieces fell into place. Each document, a fragment of reality; each photograph, a memory stilled in time. Their minds whirred, connecting dots, drawing lines.

"Are you seeing this?" Kathleen's voice rose, a note of triumph threading through her question.

"Keep going," Carmella said, resolve steeling her features. "We're piecing it together."

The moon outside cast its glow, a quiet sentinel to their unfolding discovery. They pressed on, the puzzle before them yielding its secrets one paper at a time.

Carmella's fingers hesitated, then resumed their dance through the papers. Her breath caught as she extracted a series of letters, each one more damning than the last. The ink, black and bold, bore Otto's signature at the bottom—a flourish that seemed too proud for such sinister content. She held one to the light, reading the words aloud for Kathleen's sharp ears.

"Tony, your days of subpar pizzas are numbered..." Carmella's voice trailed off, her eyes scanning the rest in silence.

"Let me see," Kathleen said, reaching for the letter. Her green eyes flicked back and forth as she read, lips moving slightly with each word. The room grew heavy with the weight of implication.

"Look at the date." Kathleen pointed. "A week before Tony...you know."

"Before he was found," Carmella filled in the gap, her wavy hair falling into her face as she nodded, a silent punctuation to Kathleen's observation.

"Otto wasn't just puffing his chest." Carmella sifted through more letters, each one echoing threats. "He had motive."

"Means, too." Kathleen added. "These letters—they're like a roadmap to what happened to Tony."

Silence fell between them. It was broken only by the distant hoot of an owl and the rustle of paper as they lined up the letters side by side, a timeline of malice unfurled on the storeroom floor.

Carmella met Kathleen's gaze, her expressive eyes fierce with resolve. They shared a moment of unspoken agreement, a contract of glances.

"We've got him," Kathleen whispered, a whisper carrying the weight of justice.

"Let's take Otto down," Carmella replied, her voice steely, the familiar twinkle of optimism now sharpened into a weapon. Together, they rose from the floor, documents in hand, ready to serve retribution as cold as the moonlight streaming through the pizzeria's windows.

Stepping out into the crisp night air, Carmella clutched the stack of papers against her chest. The full moon bathed Wavecrest Cove in a ghostly light, casting long shadows on the pavement beneath their feet. They moved quickly, the evidence burning in their hands like a torch that could ignite the truth at any moment.

"Otto won't see this coming," Kathleen said, her breath forming clouds in the chill.

Carmella nodded, her wavy hair fluttering in a passing breeze. "We'll need to be careful. He's cunning and won't hesitate to cover his tracks."

Their shoes clicked in unison against the sidewalk as they made their way back to Nonna's Slice of Heaven. The familiar scent of tomato sauce and baked dough reached them before they saw the neon sign glowing a welcome.

"Maybe we should involve Sheriff Collins," Kathleen suggested. "He'd want to know we have something solid."

"Agreed. But first thing tomorrow," Carmella replied. "Tonight, we put everything in order. We can't risk Otto getting wind of this before we're ready."

"Right." Kathleen's voice was firm. "Evidence, timeline, motive. We lay it all out for the sheriff with no room for doubt."

They paused outside Carmella's pizzeria, the old-fashioned bell above the door jingling softly as a draft caught it. Carmella looked up at the establishment her grandfather had built, feeling a surge of protective fierceness.

"Nonna's has to stay open late tonight," she declared. "I want eyes on Otto's place. If he decides to bolt..."

"I'm on it." Kathleen's reply came swift and sure. "I'll keep watch from the upstairs window. Best vantage point."

"Good." Carmella unlocked the front door, her movements quick and precise. "We'll turn the tables on him. It's our move now."

With a final glance at the moonlit street, they stepped inside, sealing themselves away from the night. The door locked behind them with a click that sounded like the cocking of a gun. Ready, aimed, and soon to be fired.

Carmella flipped on the lights, banishing shadows from the corners of Nonna's pizzeria. The familiar scent of tomato and oregano embraced them, a comforting ally in the midst of chaos. She spread the incriminating documents across a checkered tabletop, each page a piece of the puzzle they were close to solving.

"Look at this," Carmella said, tapping a photograph where Otto loomed over Tony, his finger jabbing like an accusation. "Pure intimidation."

Kathleen leaned over her shoulder, green eyes sharp. "Got him red-handed."

Their focus was surgical, piecing together timelines, motives, connections. Receipts whispered secrets of shady dealings. Letters screamed threats long silenced. They worked in tandem, Carmella's resolve mirrored by Kathleen's fierce concentration.

"Tony knew too much," Carmella murmured. "Otto couldn't risk it."

"His greed was his downfall." Kathleen's lips curled in disdain. "Thought he could control everything."

The clock ticked, relentless. Every second brought clarity. Every minute, empowerment. They were no longer two friends caught in a whirlwind of deceit; they were the storm, ready to uproot the lies that had festered for too long.

"Justice for Tony," Carmella vowed. Her voice was steel wrapped in velvet, a promise made in the heart of her grandfather's legacy.

"And your name cleared." Kathleen's agreement was a strike of flint, igniting determination.

They stood together, a united front against the dark tide of corruption. Evidence in hand, strategy set, they were armed with truth and unshakeable will.

"Let's do this," Carmella said, her words a quiet thunder rolling through the empty pizzeria.

Kathleen nodded. "For Tony."

The night outside held its breath, waiting for dawn and the justice it would usher in.

Chapter 16

Carmella's fingers traced the rim of her coffee mug, the ceramic cool under her touch. Sunlight filtered through the curtains, casting a checkerboard pattern across the living room. She glanced at Kathleen, seated opposite her on the floral-patterned couch. Worry furrowed Kathleen's brow, mirroring the unease that had settled in Carmella's stomach like a weight.

"Kathleen, I just...," Carmella began, her voice barely above a whisper. "What if we're poking a hornet's nest here?"

"Carmella, you mean with the investigation?" Kathleen leaned forward, her eyes locking onto Carmella's.

"Exactly." Carmella set down her mug, its clink against the table sounding too loud in the silence. "This isn't some petty theft or harmless prank. What if the killer takes notice? We could be targets."

Kathleen's lips pressed into a thin line. Carmella watched her friend process this, noting how Kathleen's hand paused mid-air, the humor usually dancing in her eyes now replaced with steel.

"Being targeted..." Kathleen murmured, the gravity of the situation leaving no room for her usual levity. "I hadn't let myself dwell on that."

Carmella rose and paced across the rug, her steps muffled. She stopped by the window, gazing out at the quiet street of Wavecrest Cove. It was hard to imagine danger lurking in such a peaceful place.

"Every step we take could be drawing us closer to... to who knows what," Carmella said, turning back to face Kathleen. Her heart hammered against her ribs, betraying her composed exterior.

"Carmella," Kathleen's voice was firm, pulling her gaze once more. "We need to be careful, yes. But think of what's at stake."

Carmella nodded, knowing all too well. Silence enveloped them again, each woman lost in her own troubled thoughts, the only sound the ticking of the grandfather clock, counting down seconds like a heartbeat in the quiet room.

Kathleen leaned forward, her elbows resting on her knees, eyes ablaze with a fire that defied the dimness of Carmella'sliving room. "We owe it to Tony," she said, her voice a low growl of resolve. "We owe it to ourselves. We can't let fear dictate our actions."

Carmella watched her friend, the steadiness in Kathleen's gaze, the set of her jaw. She felt a shiver run down her spine, not from cold but from the realization that retreating was never an option for Kathleen.

"Tony wouldn't have backed down," Kathleen continued, "and neither will we. We'll find out who did this—and why."

The silence returned, heavier now, as Carmella absorbed Kathleen's words. She took a slow breath, feeling the weight of generations upon her shoulders. The ticking clock seemed to echo her own pulse, a reminder of the legacy she bore.

"Kath, I..." Carmella began, her voice barely above a whisper. She paused, collecting her thoughts like scattered leaves. "What if I can't do this? What if I fail and let everything my family built fall apart?"

Her hands trembled, a rare display of uncertainty from someone usually so composed. Her gaze flickered to the framed photograph on the mantel—a black-and-white image of her grandfather outside 'Nonna's Slice of Heaven.' His smile had always been her beacon, but now doubt clouded its warmth.

"Your fear is real, Carmella," Kathleen said softly, reaching out to still Carmella's hands with a gentle touch. "But so is your strength. You've faced New York boardrooms and Wavecrest storms. This is no different."

Carmella met Kathleen's eyes. In them, she found not only conviction but also an unspoken promise of solidarity. Her breath steadied, and the shadows of insecurity receded just enough to let the glow of determination shine through once more.

Kathleen leaned in, her green eyes flickering with a spark that could light up the dimmest corners of Wavecrest Cove's mysteries. "Listen to me, Carmella," she said, her voice firm yet threaded with warmth. "You're not alone in this—never have been. We're more than friends; we're partners in every caper, every challenge life throws our way."

Carmella's hands ceased their trembling as Kathleen's words wrapped around her like a comforting shawl. The air between them hummed with shared history, unspoken understanding.

"Remember when we solved the case of Mrs. Henderson's missing cat?" Kathleen continued, a playful smile dancing on her lips. "Or the time we organized the fundraiser for the library after the storm? We did those together."

A chuckle escaped Carmella's lips, despite the gravity of their current predicament. "We did, didn't we?"

"Exactly." Kathleen's smile broadened. "We're a team. And we're going to get through this mystery just like we did with all the others—side by side."

Carmella nodded, feeling the knot in her stomach loosen. The scent of freshly brewed coffee from the kitchen wafted into the room, mingling with Kathleen's reassuring presence.

"Besides," Carmella murmured, her gaze drifting towards the window where the town lay beyond, "if we don't see this through, the consequences... they could be dire. Not just for us, but for everyone in Wavecrest Cove."

"Reputations could crumble," Kathleen agreed. "Trust in the community—shattered."

"More than that." Carmella turned back to face Kathleen, resolve hardening in her eyes. "The real killer would remain at large, and every moment we hesitate puts someone else at risk."

The ticking clock punctuated her statement, each second a reminder of the urgency pressing against them. They sat there, two silhouettes cast in the fading light, bound by the silent oath to uncover the truth. Together.

"Kathleen, think about it! The danger..." Carmella's voice cracked, tension knotting her shoulders as she paced the length of the living room rug.

"Risk is part of any investigation!" Kathleen shot back, hands landing on her hips with a decisive thud. "We can't let fear dictate our actions!"

Carmella spun around, her wavy brown hair bouncing with the abruptness of her movement. "It's easy for you to say," she said, her voice rising in pitch. "You haven't received threatening notes at your doorstep!"

"Neither have you—yet," Kathleen countered, her eyes flashing with a mix of concern and defiance. "And we'll make sure it stays that way."

The air between them hummed with unspoken worries. They stood, two friends divided by fear yet united by purpose, their breaths syncopating with the ticking clock.

"Remember when I told you about my cousin Lucy?" Kathleen's voice softened, drawing Carmella's attention. Her posture relaxed as she leaned against the back of the sofa, her green eyes holding a distant memory. "She was accused of something dreadful, something she didn't do. The whole town turned against her."

Carmella stilled, her heart reaching out to the vulnerability in Kathleen's confession. She sank into the armchair across from her friend, her defenses ebbing away.

"I was scared then too," Kathleen continued, her gaze fixed on a pattern in the carpet as if it held the secrets of the past. "But I dug deep, found evidence that cleared her name. It wasn't easy, but I couldn't let fear win."

A silent understanding passed between them. Kathleen's story, a beacon in the shadow of their ordeal, offered a glimmer of strength to Carmella's wavering spirit. Fear had gripped her, but the warmth of their friendship thawed the icy tendrils.

"Okay," Carmella breathed out, nodding slowly. Her determination, once faltering, sparked anew. Together they could face the unknown, just as Kathleen had before.

Carmella clasped her hands tightly, knuckles whitening. "It's one thing to stand by a friend," she said, her voice a thread of sound in the quiet room. "It's another to chase after shadows that might be dangerous."

Kathleen nodded, her red hair catching the late afternoon sun filtering through the window. "I know," she admitted. "But think about it, Carmella—doubt is part of being human. We can't let it paralyze us."

"True." Carmella exhaled, the tension leaving her body as she considered Kathleen's words. The clock on the mantel ticked steadily, marking the moment.

Kathleen leaned forward, elbows resting on her knees. "We're not just doing this for ourselves, are we?" she prompted. "There's justice waiting at the end of this, and if we don't pursue it, who will?"

"Justice," Carmella echoed, the word resonating within her. She felt the weight of her family's expectations, the legacy of 'Nonna's Slice of Heaven' heavy on her shoulders.

Silence settled once more, filled with the creaks and groans of the old house as it cooled from the day's heat. Carmella stood up abruptly, her chair scraping back on the wooden floor.

"Okay," she declared, her voice stronger now. "This isn't just about me, or even us. It's about setting things right." Her grandfather's lessons on integrity and courage seemed to echo through the room.

"Exactly." Kathleen's lips curved into a smile, proud and reassuring.

Carmella paced, steps sure and purposeful. "We owe it to Tony, to the town... to my grandpa." She stopped and faced Kathleen squarely. "I won't let fear dictate what I do. Or don't do."

"Good." Kathleen's agreement was simple, solid as the shelves of books she tended daily.

"Let's uncover the truth," Carmella decided, her resolve crystallizing. "For justice, for peace of mind." And with those words, an invisible mantle settled on her petite frame—a commitment to honor her family's name, to protect the life she'd chosen here in Wavecrest Cove.

Kathleen rose, her movements sharp and decisive as she approached Carmella. The light from the lamp cast a warm glow over her red hair, igniting it like autumn leaves in a sunset. "We're in this together," she affirmed, her green eyes locking onto Carmella's with an intensity that left no room for doubt. "Whatever comes our way, we'll face it side by side."

Carmella's heart pounded, not with fear but with the surge of solidarity. She nodded, drawing strength from Kathleen's unwavering support. The worries that had knotted her insides began to unravel, strand by strand.

"Your grandpa built more than a pizzeria," Kathleen continued, her voice steady and sure. "He built a community, a legacy of standing up for what's right. We're part of that now."

Carmella's lips twitched into a smile, small but genuine. Her friend's words were a balm, soothing the sting of uncertainty. She felt the resilience within her stir, coaxed to life by the promise of shared resolve.

"Thank you, Kathleen." Her voice was soft, yet it carried the weight of commitment. "I couldn't do this without you."

"Nor I without you," Kathleen replied with a quick flash of humor, breaking the tension. "Who else would keep me from diving headfirst into disaster?"

They laughed together—a momentary release from the gravity of their situation. But as the laughter faded, a silence charged with purpose settled between them.

Their gazes met once more, twin fires of determination burning in their eyes. Doubts receded, shadows cast away by the light of their combined strength. With a collective breath, they steeled themselves for what lay ahead.

The chapter closed on Carmella and Kathleen standing shoulder to shoulder, their expressions resolute. This was more than an investigation; it was a testament to their bond, to the courage that ran through their veins. Together, they would face the unknown, their conviction a beacon in the encroaching night.

Chapter 17

The phone rang, piercing the quiet of Nonna's Slice of Heaven. Carmella wiped her hands on her apron and reached for the handset, its shrill tone demanding attention. "Hello?" she answered, her voice laced with a hint of curiosity.

"Meet me," a voice crackled through static, a whisper lost in the wind. "Out past the old mill road. Alone."

"Who is this?" Carmella's brow furrowed, her grip tightening around the phone.

"Trust me," the voice urged before the line went dead.

Carmella stood motionless, the dial tone humming in her ear. She replaced the receiver, her mind racing. Her eyes met Kathleen's, who had been arranging books for the pizzeria's reading corner.

"Trouble?" Kathleen asked, sensing the tension.

"An unknown caller," Carmella said, her voice low. "Wants to meet outside of town."

"Sounds like a trap," Kathleen warned, her eyes narrowing. The air hummed with unspoken alarm.

"Or a lead." Carmella's tone held hope, her innate optimism surfacing.

"Are we considering this?" Kathleen's hand rested on her hip, her stance a blend of skepticism and readiness.

"Curiosity killed the cat," Carmella murmured, but her eyes sparkled with determination.

"Good thing we're not cats." Kathleen cracked a half-smile. "Let's go."

They grabbed their jackets, the evening chill seeping into the pizzeria. Outside, the fading sun cast long shadows across Wavecrest Cove. They drove in silence, the car's headlights cutting through the gathering dusk.

"Could be important," Carmella ventured, breaking the quiet.

"Or dangerous," Kathleen countered, her voice steady. "But we've got each other's backs."

"Always," Carmella agreed, her resolve firming. The unknown beckoned, a mystery wrapped in twilight, and together they sped towards it.

The car's engine hummed to a stop, its headlights dimming to reveal the forlorn outline of the warehouse. Gravel crunched underfoot as Carmella and Kathleen stepped out, their breaths visible in the cool night air. The parking lot lay bathed in shadows, punctuated by the occasional flicker of a streetlight struggling against the darkness.

"Here we are," Carmella whispered, her eyes scanning the desolation.

"Feels like stepping into a noir film," Kathleen remarked, pulling her jacket tighter around her.

They moved together, each step deliberate, searching for the unknown caller. The silence was thick, broken only by distant echoes that seemed to bounce off the empty building—a metallic rattle, a shiver-inducing scrape.

"Anyone here?" Carmella called, her voice louder than intended. It hung in the air, unanswered.

A shuffle came from behind a rusted dumpster. They turned sharply, hands clenched at their sides. From the penumbra stepped a figure, cautious but resolute.

"Who's there?" Kathleen demanded.

"Sorry for the dramatics," the figure replied, moving into the feeble light. His features became clear – the worn apron of Otto's pizzeria still draped over his frame, a nametag glinting dully.

"Ricky?" Carmella recognized him, a former dough-spinner from Otto's kitchen.

"Carmella, Kathleen..." He nodded, his eyes darting around nervously. "I saw it happen... the night Tony was killed."

"Otto?" Kathleen's voice was a mix of disbelief and realization.

Ricky's nod was barely perceptible, but it echoed in the stillness of the night.

Ricky shivered, not just from the cold. He glanced around once more before speaking. "It was late," he began, his voice a hoarse whisper. "The shop had closed. Tony... he came to confront Otto."

Carmella's hands were fists at her sides. She leaned in, eager for every detail.

"Words got heated," Ricky continued. "Otto accused Tony of stealing his recipes, trying to ruin him."

Kathleen frowned. "But that's absurd," she interjected. "Tony had his own style."

"Otto didn't see it that way." Ricky's eyes held a haunted look. "He said the town wasn't big enough for both of them."

"Go on," Carmella urged, her voice steady.

"Otto... he lost it. Grabbed a knife—the one he uses for slicing prosciutto." Ricky's hand mimed the arc of a blade. "Said Tony would never steal from him again."

Carmella's breath caught. Kathleen's green eyes blazed with anger and shock.

"Did anyone else know?" Kathleen asked, her voice sharp.

"Otto paid me to keep quiet. Said it was an accident, but I knew..." Ricky trailed off, shaking his head.

"Knew what?" Carmella pressed.

"Otto planned it. Waited for Tony. He wanted the competition gone."

"Thank you, Ricky," Carmella said, her voice imbued with a gravity that matched the weight of their discovery. Ricky's account, raw and unfiltered, had painted a chilling portrait of premeditation.

"Be careful," Ricky warned. "Otto's dangerous."

Carmella nodded, her resolve solidifying. "We will."

As the former employee melted back into the darkness, Carmella and Kathleen stood motionless for a moment, absorbing the enormity of what they'd learned. Ricky's words reverberated between them, stirring a storm of urgency within. They knew what had to be done next.

Carmella's heart hammered in her chest. She turned to Kathleen, the dim glow of a distant street lamp casting shadows across her friend's face. Their eyes met, and in that silent exchange, they knew - the pieces of the puzzle were finally slotting into place. The truth was within their grasp, ready to be unveiled.

"Kathleen," Carmella whispered, her voice barely rising over the hum of the wind. "We've got him."

Kathleen nodded, the corners of her mouth lifting in a determined smile. "Let's not waste another minute."

Their steps were quick and purposeful as they navigated through the gravel-strewn lot back to the car. Each crunch of stone underfoot marked their resolve. They slid into the vehicle, the leather seats cold against their skin, a stark reminder of the night's chill.

"Right to Otto's?" Kathleen asked, her hand gripping the ignition key.

"Directly," Carmella affirmed, fastening her seatbelt with a click that sounded like a starting gun. "Before he even dreams of slipping away."

The car's engine roared to life, disrupting the silence of the abandoned lot. Headlights cut through the darkness, revealing the path ahead - a path towards justice. They pulled out onto the road, the old warehouse receding into the night behind them.

"Can you believe it, Carmella? After all this time..." Kathleen's voice trailed off, her hands steady on the wheel.

"I can." Carmella's gaze was fixed on the passing scenery, each streetlight they passed bringing them closer to their confrontation. "And we'll make sure everyone else does too."

The car sped on, slicing through the stillness of the night. Otto's pizzeria loomed in their future, a showdown inevitable.

The car swerved around the bends leading to Wavecrest Cove, tires gripping the asphalt with urgency. Carmella's hands clenched in her lap, the fabric of her jeans bunching under her fingers. Kathleen's knuckles whitened on the steering wheel, each turn bringing them closer to their showdown.

"Almost there," Kathleen said, voice barely above a whisper, more for herself than for Carmella.

"Ready as I'll ever be," Carmella replied, trying to steady her breath.

They entered the town, its quaint streetlights a stark contrast to the gravity of their mission. The pizzeria sign came into view, its neon glow beckoning them to what lay ahead. They parked haphazardly, not bothering to straighten the car in its space.

"Let's do this," Kathleen uttered, and they both exited the vehicle, feet hitting the pavement in unison.

The bell above Otto's pizzeria door jangled as they pushed through, announcing their arrival. The scent of tomato sauce and melted cheese enveloped them, a comforting aroma now tainted with the stench of betrayal.

"Look for Otto," Carmella hissed, scanning the room.

He was there, behind the counter, flour dusting his apron, commanding his domain. His eyes hadn't found them yet, too busy overseeing the dance of dough and toppings.

"Carmella, there." Kathleen nodded toward him, her posture rigid.

They weaved through the tables, dodging waitstaff and patrons, two women on a singular quest. Conversations hummed around them, oblivious to the storm about to break.

Otto finally looked up, his gaze meeting theirs across the crowded room. The air seemed to thicken, charged with anticipation. Carmella'sheart drummed a relentless beat, each step forward amplifying the sound in her own ears.

"Otto Marks," Carmella called out, her voice cutting through the din.

The restaurant's clatter receded as Carmella and Kathleen closed in on Otto. Eyes fixed, they halted mere inches from the counter that separated them from him.

"Otto," Carmella's voice was steel wrapped in velvet, "we need to talk."

His frame stiffened, a deer sensing predators. His eyes darted between the two women, seeking an escape that wasn't there.

"About Tony," Kathleen added, her tone brooking no arguments.

"Tony?" Otto scoffed, feigning ignorance, but his hands betrayed him, gripping the edge of the counter like a lifeline.

"Cut the act," Carmella snapped. "We've got a witness, Otto. They saw everything."

Kathleen slapped a folded piece of paper on the counter. It fluttered like a flag of war.

"Impossible," he blurted, but his voice cracked, a glaze of sweat pearling on his brow.

"Your little scheme is over." Carmella leaned in, her gaze unyielding.

"Get out!" Otto barked, louder now, his facade crumbling. The clash of his outcry against the backdrop of clinking glasses and murmured conversations drew turned heads, slowed steps.

"Murderer," Carmella whispered, her accusation slicing through the growing stillness.

Otto's hands trembled, a stark contrast to his usual composure. His lips moved rapidly, weaving a narrative of innocence that fell flat in the charged atmosphere.

"Alibis can be faked," Carmella retorted, her tone deliberate. "But not the truth."

Kathleen unfolded the paper with a flourish, revealing a timeline that contradicted Otto's account. "You said you were at the supplier during Tony's last hours. Our witness puts you at the scene."

"Fabrications!" Otto's voice was strangled, his protest weak against their unwavering certainty.

Carmella stepped closer, her eyes narrowed. "No fabrications here. Just facts. You hated Tony for stealing your customers."

"Ridiculous!" Otto sputtered, his veneer of control cracking.

"Is it?" Kathleen's brow arched, her green eyes flashing. "Because according to this, you stood to lose more than just a few pizzas."

A hush crept over the room. The clink of cutlery ceased. Chairs scraped against the floor as patrons leaned forward, curiosity morphing into concern. The air thickened, heavy with whispers and sidelong glances.

"Everyone knew about your rivalry," Carmella pressed on, "but murder, Otto? That's a new low."

"Shut up!" Otto slammed a fist on the counter. A glass toppled, shattering on the tile. Silence followed, a collective intake of breath from the onlookers.

"Admit it," Kathleen said, her voice slicing through the quiet. "You couldn't let Tony succeed."

Eyes shifted from the shattered glass to the trio locked in confrontation. Otto's face paled, the cool strategist unmasked by his own desperation.

"Enough," Otto seethed, but his command lacked conviction. There was no turning back, not with the truth laid bare before the eyes of Wavecrest Cove.

Carmella's gaze didn't falter. "We know what you did," she said, her voice a steel thread cutting through the din of hushed voices.

Kathleen nodded, her posture rigid, an immovable force beside her friend. "The evidence is clear."

Otto's chest heaved, his breaths shallow and rapid. "You have nothing," he spat, but the quiver in his voice betrayed him.

"Wrong again." Carmella reached into her bag, fingers brushing against the crumpled pages of testimony. She held Otto's stare, letting the silence swell between them.

The scent of tomato sauce and baking dough lingered in the air, incongruously homey amid the rising tension. A child whimpered somewhere to the right, a mother's soothing shushes following.

"Think about your next move carefully, Otto," Kathleen warned. Her words were soft but carried the weight of impending justice.

Otto's hands clenched, knuckles whitening. He glanced around, seeking an ally, finding none. Every eye in the room was on him, every ear tuned to the drama unfolding.

"Tony deserved better than this," Carmella said, her tone resolute, her heart pounding against her ribs in solidarity with the truth.

"Justice will be served," Kathleen added, her green eyes reflecting the resolve that had brought them this far.

Otto's shoulders slumped, the fight draining out of him as the patrons of Wavecrest Cove witnessed the unraveling of a man they thought they knew.

Chapter 18

Carmella's fingers drummed a staccato rhythm on the worn wood of a table at Nonna's Slice of Heaven. The pizzeria was silent except for the distant hum of the refrigerator and her own sighs. Dust motes danced in the slanting afternoon light, mocking her stillness. Pizzas didn't need solving; cases did. And this case had her stumped, her spirit dwindling like the final flickers of a candle.

She eyed the door every few moments, half-expecting it to burst open with some clue, some savior from her doubts. But it remained as unmoving as her resolve. Carmella's shoulders slumped. She whispered to the empty room, "Grandpa, what would you do?"

The silence answered with echoes of past laughter and the clinking of pizza trays. She closed her eyes, breathed in the familiar scent of tomato sauce and oregano that lingered in the air. It rooted her, reminded her of countless family dinners, of her grandfather's hearty laughs and sage advice.

"Morettis don't quit," she murmured, the words a talisman against the encroaching despair. Her eyes snapped open, a fire kindled within them. She pushed back her chair with a scrape against the checkered floor and stood. Her posture straightened, a reflection of the steel in her spine.

"Okay, Carmella," she addressed herself, squaring her jaw. "Time to make Grandpa proud." Her voice, though quiet, carried the weight of newfound determination.

Carmella walked toward the counter, each step purposeful. She took one last look at the sun-dappled pizzeria – her inheritance, her home, her battleground. The warmth of the oven seemed to embolden her, chase away the chill of doubt. She grabbed her jacket from the hook by the door.

"Let's clear that name," she said, a whisper now a promise. The door's bell jingled cheerfully as she stepped out, but there was no mistaking the resolve in her stride. The case awaited, and so did her legacy.

Carmella's fingers rifled through the stack of evidence on the red-and-white checkered tablecloth, each item a puzzle piece in a confounding mystery. Photographs with timestamped corners fanned out like a hand of cards none would wish to hold. Notes scribbled in haste, their blue ink bleeding into the paper grain, lay clustered around a central newspaper clipping—the headline screamed of the murder that had shaken Wavecrest Cove.

She picked up a photograph, her gaze tracing the edges, looking for something she might have missed. The diner's neon sign was a beacon in the night, but it was the shadowy figure beneath it that held her attention. She leaned closer, the image inches from her eyes, searching for a detail that could crack the case wide open.

The bell above the pizzeria door chimed, slicing through Carmella's concentration. Detective Jones stepped inside, his tall frame momentarily blocking the light that streamed through the glass. His eyes found Carmella amid the sea of paper and images. He paused, taking in the scene: the lone woman surrounded by the detritus of an investigation.

"Quite the spread you've got there." His voice was low, respectful of the silence that had preceded him.

Carmella didn't startle; her focus barely wavered from the evidence before her. Only when he walked closer, the click of his shoes echoing off the tiled floor, did she look up. Her eyes met his—a silent exchange of acknowledgment.

"Detective," she said, her tone steady.

Jones nodded, offering a smile that softened the lines around his mouth. "I can see your head's deep in this." He gestured toward the mosaic of clues.

Carmella returned the smile tentatively, allowing herself a moment of camaraderie amidst the solitude of her task. She straightened a little, fortified by his presence. "Every piece tells part of the story," she replied. "Just trying to listen."

He glanced at the arrayed evidence again, his nod slow, approving. "Keep listening, Carmella. You're onto something."

The scent of tomato sauce lingered in the air, mingling with the faint aroma of basil and cheese from the kitchen's earlier bustle. Carmella's fingers paused over a photograph, the edges frayed with handling. Her gaze lifted to meet Detective Jones' steady blue eyes, a mix of surprise and contemplation flickering across her face.

"Thank you," she murmured, the words catching slightly as the spark of hope kindled within her. "I won't let this go unresolved."

Detective Jones acknowledged her resolve with a nod, the corner of his mouth quirking upward in a semblance of a grin. He pulled out a chair, its legs scraping against the tile floor in a sharp contrast to the hushed atmosphere. Sitting down, he leaned forward, elbows resting on the table strewn with leads and conjectures.

"Let's take a look together," he suggested, his voice firm yet inviting collaboration.

Carmella passed him a note, her hand brushing his as she did so. They poured over the details, their voices low and deliberate. "What if we've been seeing this all wrong?" she ventured, pointing to a line of text that seemed out of place.

"Could be," Jones replied, his skepticism surfacing as he tapped on another clipping. Their dialogue became a dance of theories and insights, each step drawing them closer to understanding.

Piece by piece, they challenged the puzzle before them, their partnership solidifying in the shared pursuit of truth. Each revelation, each question, wove the fabric of trust tighter between them.

Carmella's finger paused mid-air, the warmth of revelation washing over her face. Her eyes darted across the collection of photographs, then settled on a single, seemingly innocuous receipt. Detective Jones leaned in, his gaze following hers.

"Look at this timestamp," she said, her voice barely above a whisper.

Jones scrutinized the slip of paper, his brows knitting together. "It's from the morning of Tony's death. Otto claimed he was out of town."

"Exactly." Carmella's hand trembled as she pointed to the grainy background of the security camera photo pinned beside the receipt. "But that's his car, there in the corner—same day, same time."

"Outside Tony's apartment," Jones finished for her, a low growl of realization in his tone.

Excitement crackled between them like static. They exchanged a look, their shared discovery igniting a firestorm of adrenaline.

"Otto's been lying," Carmella said, her resolve firming.

"Let's make sure he can't anymore." Jones's voice was granite-hard.

They hunched over the table, piecing together their strategy. The pizzeria's ambient noises faded into the background, the scent of tomato and basil reduced to a distant memory. Their world narrowed down to facts, timelines, and the looming confrontation.

"During the Bake-off," Carmella suggested, her mind racing ahead. "He'll be there, in the public eye."

"Perfect cover." Jones nodded. "We need him off balance, confronted with evidence he can't refute."

"Publicly," Carmella added, a spark of daring in her eyes. "It'll be harder for him to squirm away."

"Agreed." He tapped a pen against the tabletop, thinking. "I'll pull in a few favors. Make sure we have everything recorded."

"Good." She straightened up, squared her shoulders. "We'll need undeniable proof."

"Let's get to work, then." Jones stood, the chair legs screeching a protest.

"Right behind you," Carmella said, her determination fueling every step. They had a truth to unravel, a legacy to uphold, and a murderer to confront.

Carmella shuffled papers, aligning them into neat stacks on the checkered tablecloth. Detective Jones leaned over, jotting notes onto a small pad, his brow furrowed in concentration. The pizzeria, once filled with the clamor of lunchtime diners, now echoed with the hush of impending justice.

"Alright," Carmella began, breaking the silence. "We need to cover all our bases before the festival." She tapped a photograph of Otto Marks. "This guy's slippery."

"Slippery, but not invisible," Jones replied. He laid out a map, dotted with locations and times. "I'll track his financials. See if there's anything dirty we can link back to Tony."

"Good idea." Carmella nodded. "I'll dig deeper into his past. There's got to be something he's hiding that tells us more about his connection to Tony."

"Meet back here at six?" Jones proposed, his voice steady.

"Six it is." Carmella agreed, her eyes alight with purpose.

They stood, and Jones extended his hand. Carmella took it, the firm grip exchanging more than just an agreement—a promise to see this through.

As the door closed behind Detective Jones, Carmella pulled on her coat. The bell above the pizzeria's entrance jingled its farewell as she stepped into the crisp outside air. Her strides were purposeful, each step a beat in the symphony of her resolve.

The library loomed ahead, its stone façade promising hidden truths within its quiet walls. Carmella pushed open the heavy door, the scent of old books welcoming her like an old friend. She made her way to the archives, every moment precious, every discovery another step towards the truth that would clear her grandfather's name and end Otto's charade.

Detective Maddox Jones pushed through the double doors of the Wavecrest Cove Police Station, the familiar buzz of radio chatter and clicking keyboards wrapping around him. His boots clicked on the polished floor, steady and resolute. He made a beeline for the records room, his blue eyes fixed.

"Back again, Maddox?" Officer Carlyle raised an eyebrow from behind the front desk, a smirk playing on his lips.

"Can't let a single thread unravel," Jones responded, his voice clipped with focus.

The records room was a haven of order, files lined in rows like soldiers at attention. Jones's hands were quick, flipping through folders, eyes scanning for anomalies. Dust particles danced in the shafts of late afternoon light as he worked tirelessly, piecing together timelines and cross-referencing statements.

Hours slipped by until he stood back, a single sheet in hand—a bank statement that didn't add up. Otto Marks had made a mistake.

Carmella's watch beeped—six o'clock. She looked up from her notes, stretched, and gathered the papers into a neat stack. Her footsteps echoed down the library's hallowed halls as she exited, anticipation tightening her chest.

They reconvened in the dimming light outside 'Nonna's Slice of Heaven,' evidence clutched like lifelines. Carmella's brown hair was tousled from hours of research, but her eyes sparkled with breakthroughs.

"Found anything?" Detective Jones asked, his tone hopeful yet guarded.

"More than I dared to hope," Carmella said, her voice a mix of fatigue and triumph. "Otto's past isn't as spotless as he'd have us believe."

Jones nodded, handing her the bank statement. "And his finances are telling their own story."

Under the glow of the streetlamp, they leaned over the hood of Jones's car, papers spread out between them. The connection was there, stark in black and white—a link from Otto to Tony, a motive hidden in plain sight.

"Looks like Otto's been funding some shady deals," Jones said, his finger tracing a line on the statement.

"Deals that Tony wanted out of," Carmella concluded, her brain firing with possibilities.

They exchanged a look, a silent acknowledgment of the gravity of their discovery. This was it—the edge of truth, the precipice of justice.

"Time to bring this to a close," Jones stated, his voice low but determined.

"Let's do it—for Tony, for Wavecrest Cove," Carmella added, her resolve steeling.

Together, they collected the papers, their partnership solidified in the shared goal. Otto Marks' days of deception were numbered. They could feel it in the air, a storm brewing, ready to break with the dawn of revelation.

Carmella turned the key in the lock, securing Nonna's Slice of Heaven for the night. The street outside was quiet, save for the distant roll of waves against Wavecrest Cove's shore. She exhaled, feeling the weight of the case pressing against her ribs like a physical burden.

"Alright, let's run through it once more," Detective Jones said, standing beside her, his posture alert, eyes sharp beneath the moonlight.

She nodded and began, "We'll need to keep an eye on Otto during the Bake-off. If he slips up..."

"Or if he contacts his silent partners," Jones interjected smoothly.

"Exactly." Carmella's voice held a new edge, tempered by the fires of their investigation.

They stood together, their reflections in the pizzeria's glass door merging into one. Trust wove through their silence, binding them with invisible threads.

"Feels like we're on the right track," Jones murmured, breaking the stillness.

"Thanks to you," she replied, meeting his gaze. Their connection was secure, built on countless hours of shared effort.

"Teamwork," he corrected gently, offering a rare smile that softened his chiseled features.

"Teamwork," she echoed, her spirits lifting.

With a final nod, they parted ways, Carmella striding toward her car, keys jangling in her determined grasp. Each step pulsed with purpose, her mind already cataloging the tasks ahead.

Detective Jones watched her go before turning on his heel, his own list of duties clear in his head. The road stretched before them both, dark yet inviting, leading to the inevitable confrontation with Otto Marks.

The night air was cool as they disappeared into separate shadows, their alliance sealed, ready to face whatever lay ahead.

Carmella's fingers danced over the keyboard, the soft clicks punctuating the stillness of the library. She delved into old records, her eyes scanning page after digital page for any mention of Otto Marks. The glow of the computer screen cast ghostly shadows across her determined face. Facts, dates, transactions—she sifted through them all, hunting for a thread to unravel his web of deceit.

"Gotcha," she whispered as a crucial piece of information caught her eye. A small inconsistency, but possibly monumental. She printed the document, the machine's hum a brief interruption in the quiet. This evidence could be the linchpin they needed.

Across town, Detective Jones sat in the dim light of the precinct's records room. Files surrounded him, towers of paper testaments to past crimes and solved cases. He rifled through folders, each movement precise. Dust particles floated in the air, disturbed by his search. His blue eyes didn't miss a beat, darting from one line of text to another. Slowly, the picture became clearer.

"Interesting," he muttered, tapping a finger on an overlooked statement. It was dated, faded, but the implications were fresh and promising. He made a copy, adding it to the growing compilation of evidence.

Both Carmella and Detective Jones were oblivious to the passage of time as they continued their separate quests. The sun dipped lower, casting a golden hue through the windows, unnoticed. They were machines of focus, fueled by the need for justice.

Later, Carmella emerged from the library, clutching a folder to her chest. Her steps were brisk, echoing off the cobblestone path. She couldn't shake the feeling of being watched, but she pushed it aside. Paranoia wouldn't help them now.

Detective Jones locked the records room, the click sounding final. He pocketed the key and strode down the hallway, his mind already plotting the next move.

Their paths would cross again soon, armed with new weapons for their arsenal. Wavecrest Cove had no idea that its tranquility would soon be shaken, its sinister underbelly exposed. But for now, Carmella and Detective Jones moved through the town, solitary figures against the encroaching night, bound by their shared goal to bring down Otto Marks.

Chapter 19

The aroma of baking dough and melting cheese permeated the air, mingling with the excited chatter of Wavecrest Cove's residents. Under the bright festoon lights, Carmella, Kathleen, and Detective Jones huddled together. They were a trio of intent amongst a sea of blissful ignorance, the thrumming energy of the festival buzzed around them.

Carmella's heart thumped in her chest, a rhythm tapping out the seconds until confrontation. She inhaled sharply, the scent of marinara sauce and oregano steadying her nerves. Her petite frame stood grounded, her eyes, pools of resolve.

"Ready?" Kathleen's voice was a soft murmur, a contrast to the revelry that surrounded them.

"Ready," Carmella whispered back, her lips barely moving.

Detective Jones gave a subtle nod, his presence a silent bulwark against the tide of people. His blue eyes scanned their immediate surroundings, an unspoken signal that it was time.

Carmella exhaled slowly, letting her breath carry away the last wisps of hesitation. The noise of the crowd dulled into a distant hum as she focused on the task at hand. Her determination radiated, a beacon that cut through the festivities like a lighthouse beam through foggy seas.

"Let's do this," she said, more to herself than to her companions. With each step toward the stage, her resolve solidified.

Kathleen fell into step beside her, a pillar of support wrapped in flowing red hair and quiet strength. Together, they moved through the crowd, unnoticed yet pivotal players in the unfolding drama of justice.

Through the throng of festival-goers, Detective Jones' gaze locked onto a figure weaving with casual arrogance. Otto Marks, his smile a blade hidden in velvet. The detective's eyes, sharp as flint, sparked with recognition and intent.

"Over there," Jones muttered, the words scarcely above the noise. His stance shifted, coiled readiness beneath the surface.

Carmella caught the signal, her feet moving before her mind fully registered the command. Her breath came quick, each step propelling her closer to destiny's edge. The murmur of the crowd became a distant river as she parted the waters of anticipation.

"Otto Marks!" Her voice, clear and bold, sliced through the cacophony. Conversations hitched, heads turned; a spotlight of sound on the man with the smug grin.

Otto paused, the mask of his smile faltering for the barest moment. Eyes met, challenge thrown and acknowledged.

Otto swiveled, a mixture of surprise and irritation flashing in his eyes. The smugness wavered but found its footing again as he faced Carmella. "Can I help you?" His voice dripped with feigned innocence.

"Actually, yes," Carmella shot back, her stance firm. She reached into her bag, fingers brushing the edges of paper that crackled with truth. With a swift motion, she produced a sheaf of documents and held them up for Otto to see.

"Recognize these?" Carmella's eyes were steel, her words clipped.

Otto's lips twitched, betraying the briefest flicker of concern before he masked it with a chuckle. "Should I?"

"Bank statements," Carmella began, the crowd's murmurs fading into a hush around them. "Phone records. And this," she tapped a photo, "is the nail in your coffin."

"Tony knew about your secret ingredient, didn't he? The one not approved by the health department." Kathleen's voice cut through from Carmella's side, steady and accusing.

Otto's composure slipped, his face tightening. He took a step forward, attempting to regain control of the narrative. "Accusations need proof," he countered, though his voice lacked its initial confidence.

"Proof?" Carmella's laugh was short, humorless. "We have receipts, Otto. Dates matching your little 'meetings' with Tony. Times when you thought no one was watching."

The crowd shifted, whispers growing like the rustle of leaves in the wind. Otto's gaze darted, seeking an ally, finding none.

"Your ambition killed Tony," Carmella declared. The papers in her hand seemed to glow with vindication. "And now, everyone knows."

Otto stood exposed, the mask of composure shattered by the weight of irrefutable evidence.

Otto's laugh was a hollow echo against the hum of the festival crowd. He waved a dismissive hand at Carmella, eyes scanning the sea of faces for a hint of doubt to exploit.

"Wavecrest Cove," he began, his voice loud, seeking to project innocence through volume. "You know me. I've served you for years. This woman,"—he pointed a well-manicured finger at Carmella—"is desperate to sully my reputation over a personal vendetta."

But the townspeople were statues, their expressions etched with unwavering support for Carmella. Their collective silence spoke volumes, denying Otto the reaction he sought.

Detective Jones moved then, a silent predator closing in. His steps were measured, his presence formidable. He halted beside Carmella, the pair a united front.

"Mr. Marks," Detective Jones said, every syllable wrapped in the cloak of authority. "Care to explain why your fingerprints were found on the inside of Tony's locked office? After hours?"

Otto's face paled. "I—I have keys. As a fellow business owner, it's not unusual—"

"Yet no one saw you that night." Jones cut him off. "And the security footage? Mysteriously erased."

A shift in the crowd, a ripple of gasps. Otto's gaze flickered, a trapped animal seeking an escape route.

"Shall we discuss the poison found in Tony's system?" Jones continued, relentless. "The same rare toxin found in your own storage?"

"Coincidence!" Otto spat the word out like a seed.

"Is it also coincidence," Jones pressed, "that your bank records show a purchase from a known supplier of such... unique ingredients?"

Otto's mouth opened, closed. No words came forth. The once smug smile had evaporated into the thickening air of accusation.

"Odd," Jones mused aloud, "how coincidences pile up around you, Mr. Marks."

A murmur rose among the townsfolk, a wave of realization cresting and breaking over the square. Otto's empire of lies crumbled beneath the weight of truth laid bare by Detective Jones.

The air crackled, thick with anticipation. Murmurs swelled from the crowd, a chorus of whispers and hushed exclamations as they leaned in, hungry for each word, each accusation that flew like sparks between Carmella, Detective Jones, and Otto Marks. Eyes darted, ears strained, the townspeople of Wavecrest Cove gripped by the unfolding drama at the heart of their beloved festival.

Carmella's chest heaved, her resolve an anchor in the tumultuous sea of faces. She took a step closer to Otto, her petite frame almost lost amid the towering stage and swelling crowd, but her spirit stood tall, unmistakable.

"Otto," she began, her voice cutting through the noise, "you can't wriggle out of this. We all deserve the truth. What did you do to Tony?"

Otto's eyes fixed on her, his cool composure a stark contrast to the fervent energy emanating from Carmella. He attempted a disdainful laugh, a hollow sound that fooled no one.

"Miss Moretti, your little theatrics are—"

"Enough games," she interjected, sharp as a knife. Her hands clenched into fists at her sides. "Tony was more than a competitor; he was part of this community. You took him from us. Why?"

Around them, the thrum of voices rose, the crowd's collective breath bated as they awaited Otto's response. The scent of tomato sauce and melted cheese, once comforting, now hung heavy, a backdrop to the bitter taste of suspicion and betrayal.

"Justice for Tony," someone called out, the words a match that lit the fuse of the community's simmering anger.

"Justice!" echoed another voice, then another, until the chant became a rallying cry that filled the square.

Otto's lips drew into a thin line, his illusion of control slipping away like oil between fingers. Carmella's gaze never wavered, her eyes two beacons of unwavering determination amidst the tempest.

"Answer me, Otto," she demanded, every syllable a hammer striking the anvil of truth. "Why did Tony have to die?"

In the midst of chaos, Carmella Moretti stood unshaken, her quest for answers a beacon that would lead Wavecrest Cove through the storm.

The crowd's murmur swelled, a sea of voices that crested with each shout of support for Carmella. "We're with you!" an elderly man barked, his fist raised high. A young mother, baby cradled in one arm, nodded vigorously, her eyes fierce with solidarity. "Justice for Tony!" The chant rippled through the gathering, a wave of communal strength that bolstered Carmella's resolve.

Mama Mia It's Murder

Otto's smugness faltered, his smirk dissolving as he registered the encircling tide of accusation. His gaze darted, seeking an ally, finding none. The townspeople, once charmed by his pizzeria's flaky crusts and secret sauces, now saw through the veneer to the corruption beneath.

"Mr. Marks," Detective Jones began, his voice slicing through the cacophony with surgical precision. All heads turned, attention snapping to the detective who stood like a lighthouse amidst the turmoil. In his hand gleamed a single key, the metal catching the afternoon sun in a silent accusation. "Care to explain why this was found at the crime scene?" Jones asked, his tone deceptively mild.

Otto's eyes locked onto the key, recognition flashing across his features before he could shutter it behind bravado. The crowd leaned in, breaths held, the collective pulse of Wavecrest Cove quickening.

"Found where you left it, in Tony's prep room," Jones continued, unwavering. "Your fingerprints, Otto. No escaping that."

The sea of faces around them shifted, the undercurrent of doubt swept away by the hard fact that tethered Otto inexorably to the act. Otto's mouth opened, closed, no words forthcoming, his composure shattered by the relentless tide of truth.

Carmella watched, heart thundering in her chest, as the reality of their victory began to dawn. Detective Jones had played his part flawlessly, the final piece of evidence laid bare for all to see. Otto Marks, once a pillar of the community, now stood isolated, exposed by the light of justice that Maddox Jones had promised to deliver.

A cheer surged from the crowd, a wave of sound that carried the weight of justice and relief. Otto's face, once the portrait of smug assurance, crumbled as the reality of his situation pressed down upon him like the heat of an oven set too high. His eyes, cold and calculating, now darted around frantically, seeking an escape that didn't exist.

Detective Maddox Jones's keen eyes sliced through the crowd. A flash of a crisp white shirt, the edge of tailored pants—Otto Marks was making a break for it. The Best Pizzeria Bake-off Festival buzzed with excitement, but Maddox's focus narrowed, his senses sharpening as he zeroed in on his quarry.

Otto weaved like a ghost among the festival-goers. Laughter and chatter filled the air, the aroma of baking dough and melting cheese thick enough to taste. Otto's figure flickered between families and vendors, near the vibrant tents that housed the competition's heart.

Maddox pushed off from his post against a lamppost. His stride was quick, purposeful. Each step carried the weight of justice, of untold stories needing an end. He sidestepped a child chasing a runaway balloon, her giggles slicing through the din. A group of teenagers, selfie-absorbed, barely noticed as Maddox slipped past them, his gaze locked on the retreating back of the pizzeria owner.

"Excuse me," he murmured, his voice barely disturbing the festival's hum as he maneuvered around a couple engrossed in choosing the perfect slice. His dark hair, short-cropped, was a shadow darting through the sea of people; his eyes stayed fixed on Otto's retreat.

Otto's pace quickened, the gap between him and freedom shrinking with every hurried step. But Maddox was faster, more determined. His years in the city had honed his ability to navigate crowds—a skill proving invaluable now, in the pursuit of truth.

He closed in, the distance between detective and suspect diminishing with each heartbeat. Maddox's breath remained even, his mind clear. He was the hunter, the seeker of answers in a world where questions multiplied like shadows at dusk.

Otto's shoulder brushed a table laden with trophies, nearly sending a golden pizza cutter award clattering to the ground. An apology hung unsaid as he pressed on, but Maddox saw the momentary stumble, the flaw in the rhythm of escape.

The detective surged forward, his body a silent promise of impending capture. Otto's silhouette loomed nearer, the finish line of his flight now just a whisper away. But Maddox was closer, the threads of fate drawing taut between them.

Otto's head snapped back, a fleeting glance that caught the steely determination in Maddox's gaze. Panic flared in his eyes, the whites stark against the backdrop of fleeing figures. His breath hitched, body tensing as if ready to bolt from some unseen predator.

"Otto Marks!" Maddox's voice cut through the cacophony, slicing the air with authority. "Stop right there!"

The words ricocheted off the food stands and echoed in the ears of startled onlookers. Otto's stride faltered, his flight momentarily grounded by the gravity of that command.

"Hands where I can see them," Maddox demanded, his tone leaving no room for negotiation. The detective's hand hovered over his holster, a silent warning etched into the very set of his shoulders.

Otto's legs churned with raw urgency. Each step a silent plea for freedom. The crowd, once an amiable throng of festival-goers, now transformed into obstacles in his high-stakes race. He nudged shoulders, sidestepped a stroller, his every movement a dance of desperation. Sweat beaded on his brow, his breath ragged as he navigated the human maze.

Maddox kept pace. A predator in pursuit. His boots thumped against the pavement, a steady drumbeat to Otto's erratic heart. Eyes locked on the fleeing figure, he dodged a laughing child, skirted a cluster of chatting friends, never losing sight of his quarry. His breath formed clouds in the cool air, each one a testament to his relentless chase.

"Enough, Marks!" Maddox bellowed over the noise. His voice did not waver; it demanded attention.

Otto's head jerked at the sound but he did not slow. Instead, he pushed harder, elbows sharp as blades, carving a path through the mass of bodies.

Maddox matched his acceleration. Instinct and training propelled him forward, his focus narrowed to the space between him and Otto. His jacket flapped behind him, the fabric whispering secrets of justice soon to be served.

"Otto!" Maddox called again, louder, closer. "It's over!"

But the words were just wind to Otto, who ran as though hell itself snapped at his heels.

Otto's gaze flickered ahead, zeroing in on salvation: an alleyway. Its narrow mouth gaped between two brick buildings, an escape route from the encroaching lawman. He veered sharply, his shoes skidding on loose gravel as he launched himself towards the opening.

"Got you now," Maddox muttered under his breath, eyes catching Otto's sudden shift in direction. Wisdom of the streets and countless pursuits whispered to him, guiding his next move. Without hesitation, he broke left, slipping between a hot dog vendor and a cluster of tourists snapping photos.

The crowd closed behind him like water, unaware of the chase that sliced through its current. Maddox emerged at the alley's entrance just as Otto's silhouette dissolved into shadows. The detective's boots hit the ground with purpose. Each step a declaration: not this time, not on my watch.

"Otto!" His voice echoed off the walls, sharp and unyielding. "End of the line!"

Dust swirled. Shadows clung to the crumbled walls of the alleyway where Detective Maddox Jones now stood, his eyes scanning for any hint of movement. The stench of refuse and the distant echo of festival music barely registered as he honed in on the task at hand. Every rustle, every shift in the dim light could betray Otto's location.

"Come out, Otto," Maddox's voice sliced through the silence, a calm, even threat that bounced off the bricks and into the hidden crevices.

Otto Marks, from his unseen vantage point, felt his heart hammer against his ribcage. Desperation seeped into his calculated mind. Eyes wild, he scoured the alley's dead ends, the fire escapes just out of reach, the barred windows offering no respite. Trapped. Options dwindled with each passing second.

Maddox advanced, steps silent on the pavement. Instincts sharpened over years whispered caution; his training, a map of possible outcomes. He observed the slight disturbances in the dust, the faint prints leading deeper into the alley's throat.

"Running only makes things worse," he called out again, his tone unyielding yet devoid of malice.

A cat yowled somewhere high above, and a trash can lid clattered to the ground, giving away Otto's frantic search for an escape. Maddox moved towards the sound, a predator certain of his prey. Otto's breath hitched as he pressed further into the shadows, understanding the futility of evasion.

"Otto," Maddox said, one last offer wrapped in the inevitability of capture. "It's time."

The alley held its breath as two minds, hunter and hunted, reached the inevitable conclusion of their deadly game.

Maddox's gaze cut through the darkness, unrelenting. Shadows played tricks, but not on him. A subtle shift behind wooden crates snagged his attention. There—Otto Marks, a figure of panic, crouched and cornered.

"Found you," Maddox whispered to himself, satisfaction fleeting.

He edged closer, boots silent against the gritty ground. Each step measured, deliberate. Otto's chest heaved in ragged synchrony with the detective's advance. The air hung thick with fear and the stale tang of refuse.

"Otto." Maddox's voice held no tremor, only certainty.

Mama Mia It's Murder

Blue eyes, twin mirrors of Maddox's own, flickered up. Recognition. Defeat. Otto's glasses slipped down his nose, forgotten. He adjusted them out of habit, hands quivering.

"Detective Jones," he managed, voice barely above a murmur.

"Stay where you are," Maddox commanded. His hand hovered over his holster, a silent threat etched in muscle memory.

Otto nodded, a mere bob of his head, understanding the futility of further resistance. Maddox closed in, senses alert for any last-ditch effort to flee. The moment stretched, taut as a wire.

"Let's end this now," Maddox said, his tone final.

Otto's arms lifted. His surrender slow, deliberate. Palms facing outward, they trembled in the dim light—a silent testament to his defeat.

"Okay," he stuttered, "okay, I did it—I killed Tony."

The confession hung heavy in the air, a grim shadow flitting across Maddox's resolute face. Otto's voice continued, quivering with each syllable, sketching the outline of his guilt.

"Tony... he was going to ruin me. I couldn't let that happen."

Maddox nodded, his blue eyes reflecting none of the turmoil surely raging within Otto. He stepped forward, the distance between justice and its due shrinking with every footfall.

"Hands on the wall," Maddox instructed.

Otto complied, the bricks cold and unyielding against his fingertips. Maddox retrieved cuffs from his belt, the metallic click breaking the alley's silence as they secured Otto's wrists. They were firm, unbreakable—like the detective's resolve.

"Walk," Maddox said, his grip on Otto's arm guiding but firm.

Together, they moved through the shadows, footsteps echoing off the walls. The alley released them back into the festival's cacophony, the scent of baking dough and simmering sauce stark against the alley's dankness. Otto's head bowed, his fate sealed, and Maddox, ever vigilant, led him through the throngs of oblivious revelers.

Detective Maddox Jones stepped into sunlight, Otto Marks in tow. The festival's din hushed, an invisible ripple quieting the crowd. Heads turned. Eyes widened. Whispers died on lips. A path cleared, as if by unspoken agreement, through the sea of spectators.

Carmella Moretti stood near the pizza ovens, flour dusting her apron. Her gaze locked onto the procession, relief and vindication blooming across her face. She straightened, shoulders back, a silent warrior's stance after a long-fought battle.

"Is that...?" someone murmured.

"Otto? But why?"

Maddox ignored them, his grip on Otto unyielding. He walked, each step measured, purposeful. The clink of handcuffs punctuated the silence, a stark reminder of the gravity of their exit.

Otto's head hung low, defeat etched in the sag of his shoulders. His glasses caught the light, momentarily shielding his eyes before he looked up. There was no denying now, no room for doubt.

"Carmella," Maddox called out, his voice carrying over the stillness. "It's over."

Carmella nodded, her expression softening as she crossed the distance. The crowd parted further, granting her passage. Her eyes met Maddox's, gratitude mingling with newfound strength.

"Thank you," she said, simple, heartfelt.

The crowd remained silent, a collective breath held. They watched as Maddox led Otto past the vibrant banners and festive tables, away from the heart of the community he'd betrayed.

"Justice," someone whispered.

"Finally," another agreed.

And then, slowly, applause burgeoned, starting with a single pair of hands and spreading like wildfire. It rose in volume, a thunderous approval, a community's release.

Carmella turned to face the crowd, her smile bright. Wavecrest Cove had found its peace, and with it, so had she.

Chapter 20

Carmella's eyes fluttered open to the soft light of dawn seeping through the gauzy curtains. The quiet hum of Wavecrest Cove greeted her, a stark contrast to the cacophony of New York City mornings she once knew. She stretched, her muscles welcoming the new day with that eager anticipation that had become her morning ritual.

With swift movements, Carmella slipped from the warmth of her bed and into the clothes she'd laid out the night before. A pair of well-worn jeans hugged her petite frame; a crisp, white shirt draped over her like a promise of the day's potential. Her short, wavy brown hair fell just right without fuss, as if it too understood the demands of her new life.

Downstairs, the pizzeria beckoned. The lock clicked softly behind her as she stepped into her grandfather's legacy. The scent of baking dough enveloped her, a fragrant welcome that never failed to coax a smile onto her lips. The ovens' steady hum was music to her ears, the prelude to the symphony of a busy day ahead.

She rolled up her sleeves, her bare arms embracing the warmth of the kitchen. Flour dusted the air, settling lightly on her skin as she scooped a generous portion onto the worn wooden countertop. Carmella's hands dove into the dough, strong and confident. Each press and turn was a testament to her dedication, each fold a step closer to honoring the family name etched into every brick of Nonna's Slice of Heaven.

"Morning glory to you," she whispered to herself, a hint of her advertising days lingering in the catchy phrase. But here in Wavecrest Cove, the slogans held more truth than artifice. Here, her words were as much a part of her as the pizzas she crafted with love and care.

Carmella's hands worked the dough, pushing and folding with a rhythmic grace. The coolness of the countertop seeped through the flour, grounding her in the moment. She lost herself in the motion, a dance passed down through generations.

At a nearby table, two voices bubbled with excitement, punctuating the symphony of kitchen sounds. Carmella's ears tuned to the chatter as she continued her task.

"Wavecrest Cove's Bake-off Festival is this weekend," one customer said, his voice tinged with anticipation. "I can't wait to try what Nonna's Slice of Heaven is bringing to the table."

"Absolutely," chimed the other, "Carmella's been shaking things up. It'll be the highlight for sure!"

A smile crept onto Carmella's face, unseen by the patrons but felt deep within her chest. Her fingers pressed a final time into the soft mound of dough before her. Pride swelled. The festival was more than an event; it was a stage for her dreams and efforts.

With each pat of her hand, determination grew. She would not only attend the festival but stand out. Nonna's Slice of Heaven was hers to wield, her story to tell through a tapestry of flavors.

"Thank you," she murmured to the air, the words meant for the customers but kept close, a silent affirmation of her resolve. Carmella's gaze flickered to the oven, its steady heat a promise of triumphs ahead.

Sunlight streamed through the pizzeria windows, casting a warm glow on the countertops as Carmella wiped her flour-dusted hands on her apron. The bell above the door jingled, heralding the arrival of Mayor Edna Perkins. She entered with a flourish, her silver bob glinting and her arms cradling a basket brimming with colorful produce.

"Morning, Carmella!" Edna's voice rang out, clear and cheerful.

"Mayor Edna," Carmella greeted, noting the fresh vegetables. "What brings you here?"

"Gifts from my garden," Edna said, placing the basket on the counter. "Zucchinis, tomatoes, peppery arugula—perfect for your pizzas."

"Thank you. These are wonderful," Carmella replied, inhaling the scent of ripe tomatoes.

Edna leaned forward, her glasses catching the light. "Wavecrest Cove thrives when we all chip in. It's how we've always done things around here."

"Community makes this place special," Carmella agreed, feeling a kinship with the town that had embraced her so warmly.

"Remember that at the festival," Edna added with a wink before sweeping back out the door.

Carmella pondered Edna's words as she turned off the oven and hung her apron. The streets beckoned, alive with the hum of daily life. She strolled past storefronts, each a small world of charm and history. Locals waved, calling out greetings that Carmella returned with a smile.

The library's familiar musty scent enveloped her as she pushed open the door. Inside, Kathleen stood amidst stacks of books, her red hair a bright beacon.

"Carmella! Look what I found," Kathleen exclaimed, waving a thick volume. "A culinary history of Wavecrest Cove!"

"Any pizza secrets?" Carmella teased, leaning over the open pages.

"Maybe one or two," Kathleen replied, her eyes twinkling. "But it's the stories, Carmella. Our town's love for food runs deep."

"Let's make history then," Carmella said, her mind already dancing with possibilities.

"Let's," Kathleen agreed, her laughter echoing off the shelves as they delved into the book together.

Papers rustled, pages flitted under eager fingers as Carmella and Kathleen hunched over the heavy tome. "What about a clam and garlic white pizza?" Carmella suggested, tapping a black-and-white photograph of fishermen at the cove.

"Or a lobster thermidor topping?" Kathleen countered. "Too fancy?"

"Wavecrest Cove's not shy about seafood," Carmella mused, picturing the colorful crustaceans from local waters atop a golden crust.

"Let's add some zest to tradition," Kathleen said, scribbling notes.

"Maybe a hint of lemon," Carmella added, excited by the culinary challenge.

"Perfecto!" Kathleen exclaimed, clapping her hands. Their laughter mingled with the scent of aged books.

With ideas simmering, Carmella returned to Nonna's Slice of Heaven. The bell above the door jingled as she stepped inside, her sanctuary of sauce and dough beckoning. She dusted flour across the counter, every movement a step closer to victory at the festival.

"Carmella Moretti!" boomed a voice that could only belong to Frankie "The Dough" Marino.

"Frankie!" Carmella turned, surprised to see the robust man in her kitchen. "To what do I owe the pleasure?"

"Got a gift for ya," he said, presenting an old, stained notebook. "Marino family's secret sauce recipe."

"Really?" Carmella's heart raced. An offering like this didn't come lightly.

"Let's cook," Frankie declared, rolling up his sleeves.

They set to work, chopping fresh herbs, crushing plump tomatoes, tasting and tweaking. Frankie's hands moved with practiced ease, his laugh rich and full as he shared stories of his nonna's kitchen. Carmella followed, learning, laughing, feeling the bond of shared secrets fortifying.

"More basil," Frankie instructed after a taste test.

"Touch more garlic," Carmella countered, gaining confidence.

"Brava," Frankie nodded, approving her instincts.

The afternoon waned as they perfected the sauce, a symphony of sizzle and spice filling the pizzeria. In the end, they stood side by side, Frankie drizzling the thick, aromatic sauce onto a waiting circle of dough.

"Here's to Nonna's Slice of Heaven," he toasted, lifting a spoon. "May it shine at the festival."

"Thanks to you, Frankie," Carmella said, gratitude warming her tone.

"Family helps family," Frankie replied, his smile saying more than words ever could.

As the sun dipped low, the air in Nonna's Slice of Heaven hummed with promise. A new recipe, a cherished bond, and a festival on the horizon—Carmella was ready.

Carmella wiped the counter with a sigh, her gaze drifting through the steam-fogged windows of Nonna's Slice of Heaven. The sun dipped behind the quaint rooftops of Wavecrest Cove, casting a soft golden light across the pizzeria's checkered floor. She paused, hands still, and let the moment sink in—a moment to take stock, to breathe.

"Quite the day, huh?" came a voice from the doorway.

She turned to see Mayor Edna, her silver bob glinting in the dusk, an array of vibrant scarves wrapped around her neck.

"More than I could've imagined," Carmella admitted, a smile finding its way onto her lips. Her eyes met Edna's—there was recognition there, an understanding that went beyond words.

"Your grandfather would be proud," Edna said, offering a gentle nod. "The whole town's buzzing about your sauce."

"Thanks to Frankie—and you. Your support means everything." Gratitude softened Carmella's expression as she leaned against the wooden counter.

"Speaking of which," Greta Olsen chimed in, emerging from the throng of tables with her trademark inquisitive look. "I hear there's a celebration brewing?"

Carmella chuckled, sharing a knowing glance with Greta. "Thought we'd have a little gathering. Tonight. A thank-you for all the encouragement."

"Count me in," Greta stated, her voice bubbling with excitement. "Wouldn't miss it for the world."

"Invite the usual suspects," Carmella instructed, her tone playfully conspiratorial. "Let's show them what gratitude tastes like."

"Will do," Greta replied, already reaching for her phone, her fingers dancing over the keys in anticipation.

Edna clapped her hands, the sound echoing off the tile. "A party? How delightful! I'll bring the wine."

"Nonna's Slice of Heaven is more than just a name—it's a promise," Carmella mused aloud, watching her friends spring into action, their energy infectious.

"Indeed," Edna agreed with a wink. "And tonight, we celebrate that promise."

The pizzeria filled with the scents of baking dough and simmering sauce, the sounds of laughter and chatter a prelude to the evening ahead. Carmella's heart swelled with pride for her work, her legacy, and the community she now called family.

Glasses clinked. Warm light bathed the cozy interior of Nonna's Slice of Heaven. The pizzeria hummed with life, a symphony of joy and camaraderie. Carmella moved through the room, her laughter mingling with the melodies of conversation that danced in the air. A plate of her signature pizza made its way from table to table, its aroma a testament to the care woven into every ingredient.

"Your grandfather would be proud," Mayor Edna said, raising her glass in a toast. "To Carmella, who's brought new life to this old place."

"Here, here!" echoed Greta Olsen, her eyes bright with mirth.

Carmella's heart brimmed as she surveyed the scene; these faces had become her anchors in a once-foreign sea. Their smiles were her lighthouse, their stories her map. She had navigated uncertainty and found her harbor.

"Thank you, all of you," Carmella replied, her voice steady yet imbued with emotion. "This is home because you're all in it."

Nods and murmurs of agreement rippled through the group. They ate, they drank, they shared tales of Wavecrest Cove's past, intertwining them with hopes for the future.

The evening waned, shadows stretching across the checkered floor. Laughter softened to contented sighs. Embers of friendship glowed in the dimming light. Carmella began the familiar ritual of closing—wiping down tables, turning off lights, the click of the lock a comforting punctuation.

Outside, the moon lit her path, a silent sentinel for her thoughts. A gentle breeze carried the salt-kissed whispers of the cove, and Carmella walked with a buoyant step. Her spirit was anchored, her resolve unshaken. She had weathered the storm of change, and now, the calm waters of belonging cradled her dreams.

Nonna's Slice of Heaven stood dark and still behind her, a monument to what she had achieved—a beacon for what was yet to come.

Chapter 21

Carmella wove through the throng of festival-goers, her senses alive to the crackle of crust and the tangy zip of tomato sauce in the air. Detective Maddox Jones stood like a beacon amidst the chaos, his eyes finding hers across the sea of bobbing heads. The Best Pizzeria Bake-off Festival had transformed Wavecrest Cove into a carnival of culinary delight, but for Carmella, the only thing that mattered now was the man who had become her unexpected ally in more ways than one.

"Quite the turnout," Maddox remarked as Carmella reached him, his voice steady over the hum of conversation.

"Nonna's Slice would have loved this," she replied, the pride for her grandfather's pizzeria infusing her words.

The corner of Maddox's mouth twitched upward, acknowledging her dedication. They stood shoulder to shoulder, watching as children darted between stalls, their laughter mingling with the clinks of glasses and the occasional cheer from the crowd.

Carmella's gaze drifted back to Maddox, and she caught the tail end of a smile before his detective mask slid back into place. Those blue eyes of his seemed to flicker with a shared secret, holding her in a momentary trance. She stepped closer, her pulse quickening, fingers quivering ever so slightly at her side.

"Did you—?" she began, but her voice trailed off, lost to the sudden swell of noise as a local band struck up a tune nearby.

Maddox leaned in, his head tilting toward her. "You okay?"

She nodded, swallowing the flutter in her throat. "Yeah. Just... it's a lot."

"Understandable." His words were simple, but they carried weight, reassurance wrapped within the layers of his quiet observation.

Carmella let out a breath she hadn't realized she'd been holding. Here, in the eye of the storm that was the festival, with the scent of oregano and cheese wrapping around them, she found an unexpected calm in Maddox's presence. And perhaps, just maybe, a hint of something more.

Detective Jones extended his hand, the rough pad of his thumb caressing the softness of Carmella's cheek. His touch was a whisper, yet it roared through her senses. Their gazes interlocked, an unspoken pact igniting in the space between them.

"Carmella," he murmured, the timbre of his voice grounding yet somehow elevating her.

Her eyelids fluttered, and she inhaled sharply, the mingled scents of basil and tomato sauce enveloping them. Maddox's face drew nearer, his breath warming her skin. Inches apart, their lips poised in hesitation, the festival crowd became a distant hum. Time curled around them, holding its breath.

Carmella's heart thundered, her breath a whisper against Detective Jones' lips. She closed the gap, her lips meeting his with a tenderness that belied the firm resolve beneath. The kiss was soft, an affirmation of shared struggles and triumphs, of late-night stakeouts and early morning briefings that had woven their lives together in the most unexpected of ways.

Maddox responded in kind, his hand finding the small of her back, pulling her closer. Their passion, held at bay by professionalism and the pursuit of justice, now flowed freely, a river breaking through a dam.

The crowd's cheers crescendoed around them, the vibrant energy of the Best Pizzeria Bake-off Festival amplifying each clap and whistle. They had done more than solve a case; they had captured the heart of Wavecrest Cove. The townspeople, who had watched Carmella grow from the newcomer with big-city ideas to the pizzeria owner who fought for her grandfather's legacy, now celebrated not just the end of danger but the beginning of love.

"Way to go, detective!" someone shouted from the throng, the title echoing with a warmth usually reserved for friends rather than law enforcement.

"Nonna's Slice of Heaven has its angel," another voice chimed in, laughter lilting through the words.

Carmella and Maddox remained locked in their embrace, the world around them a blur of exuberance and festivity. In this moment, it was just Carmella and Maddox, two hearts entwined by fate and a kiss that tasted of promise and pepperoni.

Carmella's lips parted from Maddox's, their breaths mingling in the cool evening air. A smile played on her lips, echoed by the soft upturn of his mouth. In their gaze, a tapestry of joy and relief wove itself, each thread a tale of close calls and narrow escapes. They knew, without words, that the pages of their story were just beginning to turn.

"Wow," Carmella exhaled, her voice a whisper against the backdrop of applause.

"Indeed," Maddox replied, his usual skepticism replaced by something lighter, hopeful.

Carmella's hand reached for his, fingers sliding between his with ease. Their hands fit together as if molded from the same clay. They turned, stepping in unison through the festival. The aroma of basil and mozzarella filled the air, a savory reminder of the community they had fought to protect.

Around them, friends and neighbors waved, their smiles broad and genuine. Chuck, the postman, tipped his cap, his grin nearly splitting his face. Betty, who ran the flower shop, clapped her hands, her laughter like bells in the wind.

"Couldn't have scripted it better," Carmella whispered, her advertising mind never far away.

"Life often writes the best stories," Maddox mused, his eyes reflecting the twinkle of string lights above.

Together, they navigated the sea of tables and tents, the sense of belonging wrapping around them like a warm shawl. Wavecrest Cove had become more than a place; it was home, a canvas where their love and lives would continue to unfold.

They strolled between the rows of vibrant booths, laughter and chatter enveloping them like a warm blanket. Suddenly, a figure in bright attire emerged from the crowd. Mayor Edna Perkins approached, her silver bob catching the sunlight.

"Carmella, Detective Jones!" she exclaimed, her voice carrying over the din. "Bravo on cracking that case, and what a delightful surprise this romance is!"

"Thank you, Mayor Perkins," Carmella said, feeling Maddox's hand tighten around hers.

"Wavecrest Cove owes you both a debt of gratitude," Edna continued, her glasses glinting mischievously. "And to celebrate, I'll personally bake you my special four-cheese pizza. It's legendary, you know."

Maddox chuckled. "We look forward to it, Mayor."

Before another word could be spoken, Greta Olsen slipped through the throng, her excitement as palpable as the aroma of oregano in the air. "Carmella, Maddox! We must have a party at the inn. Pizza, music, dancing—I'll organize everything!"

"Sounds perfect, Greta," Carmella replied, her heart still racing but now also filled with warmth.

"Let's make it a night Wavecrest Cove will never forget," Greta declared, clapping her hands together with a decisive snap.

"Agreed," Maddox nodded, his blue eyes sparkling with anticipation. "A celebration it shall be."

Carmella's gaze met Maddox's, a silent conversation passing between them. Her eyes, usually so full of resolve, now shimmered with something softer, more vulnerable—a reflection of their shared journey. His nod, subtle yet certain, spoke of his own acceptance into this seaside community that had become much more than just a backdrop for his investigations.

The festival swirled around them, a kaleidoscope of color and sound. Children darted past, their laughter mingling with the strumming of a guitar somewhere in the distance. The scent of basil and mozzarella lingered on the breeze, an aromatic anchor amidst the sea of festivities.

"Feels like home, doesn't it?" Carmella whispered, her words barely audible over the hum of conversation.

"More than I ever imagined," Maddox replied, his voice steady as he squeezed her hand.

They stepped forward together, joining a group of locals by a booth adorned with strings of twinkling lights. A slice of pizza found its way into each of their hands, the cheese still bubbling from the oven's embrace. As they took a bite, flavors exploded on their tongues—tangy tomato, rich cheese, the perfect char on the crust.

"Here's to new beginnings," Carmella said, raising her slice in a toast.

"New beginnings," echoed Maddox, clinking his pizza against hers with a smile.

Around them, the festival pulsed with life. Couples swayed to the music, friends laughed over shared meals, and the future stretched out before Carmella and Detective Jones, ripe with possibility. They were part of Wavecrest Cove now, woven into the town's fabric as surely as the threads of a well-loved quilt.

Together, they moved through the crowd, absorbing the joy, the camaraderie, the simple pleasure of being alive in this moment. With each step, they wrote the first lines of a new chapter—one filled with mystery, adventure, and a love that had blossomed in the most unexpected of places.

Patti Petrone Miller

About the Author

      Ladies and gentlemen, step right up to "Where the Magic Happens" - a literary circus that'll make your bookshelf do backflips!
Meet Patti, the ringmaster of this wordy wonderland! She's not just an Executive Producer; she's a word-wrangling wizard, conjuring up an animated TV series based on "ELLIOT FINDS A HOME." It's the tail-wagging tale of a thumbs-up pup and his silent sidekick, proving that you don't need words when you've got opposable digits and a heart of gold!

Hold onto your bestseller lists, folks! This Polygon Entertainment superstar has hit the USA TODAY jackpot and Amazon's #1 spot more times than a cat has lives. With 7 dozen books under her belt, she's got more genres than a chameleon has colors. From Urban Fantasy to Horror, she's been spinning yarns longer than your grandma's knitting needles!

But wait, there's more! Patti's life is like a celebrity bingo card:

She rocked "Romper Room" at 4, probably making the other kids look like amateur rompers.

She rubbed elbows with Captain Kangaroo and Mr. Green Jeans. (No word on whether the jeans were actually green.)

She shared a train ride and a sandwich with Sidney Poitier. Talk about a meal ticket to stardom!

Mama Mia It's Murder

She high-fived President Nixon at the circus. Who knew the circus could get any more political?

She went to school with David Copperfield. We assume she didn't disappear during attendance.

She roller-skated with pre-famous John Travolta. Grease lightning, indeed!

She sipped cocoa with Abe Vigoda. Fish never tasted so sweet!

When she's not busy being a literary legend, Patti's juggling roles faster than a circus performer. Teacher, grandma, furparent - she does it all with a smile that could light up a haunted house.

Speaking of haunted houses, meet the "Queen of Halloween" herself! This Wiccan High Priestess is stirring up stories spookier than a skeleton's dance moves. Her books are flying off the shelves faster than witches on broomsticks, so follow her on social media or risk missing out on the hocus-pocus!

So, come one, come all, to Patti's phantasmagorical world of words! It's more exciting than a roller coaster, more magical than a rabbit in a hat, and more diverse than a box of assorted chocolates. Don't be shy - step into the spotlight and join the literary party where the pages turn themselves and the stories never end!

www.ingramcontent.com/pod-product-compliance
Lightning Source LLC
LaVergne TN
LVHW041949070526
838199LV00051BA/2960